Hope you enjoy reading this. I certainly enjoyed writing it.

Tea, Love & Suspicion

Audrey

by Audrey Taylor-Smith

Copyright © 2013 by Audrey Taylor-Smith

First Edition – November 2013

ISBN

978-1-4602-1772-6 (Hardcover)

978-1-4602-1773-3 (Paperback)

978-1-4602-1774-0 (eBook)

All rights reserved.

No part of this publication may be reproduced in any form, or
by any means, electronic or mechanical, including photocopying,
recording, or any information browsing, storage, or retrieval
system, without permission in writing from the publisher.

Produced by:

FriesenPress

Suite 300 – 852 Fort Street
Victoria, BC, Canada V8W 1H8

www.friesenpress.com

Distributed to the trade by The Ingram Book Company

CHAPTER ONE

I left work early, it was almost eleven o'clock. I would have lunch when I got to Jenna. It was a beautiful day, hardly a cloud in the sky. I was looking forward to the drive and having my tires changed. Not exactly the thrill of a lifetime for most but I had been waiting for three weeks to have my tires and rims shipped to my friends shop. George had phoned to let me know that they had arrived.

I had gone to school with George and he was a dear and trusted friend. I planned on being early so I could visit with George's parents and enjoy a leisurely lunch.

I had hated the small tires on my new car almost from the first day I bought it. Changing them had now become an obsession. I thought I could get used to them but every time I walked to my car I thought the tires were flat.

George thought I was crazy but he knew better than to argue with me." It's so expensive." He had said. "The tires look good on your car." I didn't care how much it cost, they didn't look good to me, so they had to be changed.

We had a local repair shop in my own town but I had always taken my vehicles to George. It was only an hour drive through the mountain to the sleepy town of Jenna where he had his shop. It was a good excuse to have a visit.

I must have been about eight miles outside of Jenna when the sky suddenly turned an ugly yellowish brownish black. Out of nowhere came a rain that took my breath away. I could feel myself suck in air as if it was the last chance I would get.

Within seconds it was as if the skies had opened up and dumped every last drop of water it had left. It was pounding on my car so hard I couldn't even hear my radio. My ears were popping like popcorn and I had a horrible feeling things were going to get worse.

CHAPTER TWO

The road had literally disappeared so I slowed to a crawl. I hadn't noticed any car lights ahead of me nor behind. I felt like I was the only one who was witness to this freak of nature. My wipers were totally useless. All I knew for sure was that there was a huge drop off on my right side and the mountain to my left, so I kept a little to the left.

Without warning there was the loudest clap of thunder I had ever heard. The car lifted off the road and was brutally thrown back down. Simultaneously there was a streak of lightning that blinded me. Everything was white and I could feel the heat.

I hit the brakes and stopped.

Maybe I had been struck by lightning. All of a sudden I thought about my wimpy tires. I thought for sure I had felt the rims hit pavement. I was terrified. I had heard that you should stay in your car during a thunder storm, the tires are insulators. But the tires I had on my car didn't make me feel safe at all.

My foot couldn't put pressure on the gas pedal I was shaking so badly. My hands had gripped the steering wheel so hard I couldn't let go. I closed my eyes, put my head on the steering wheel and prayed.

I must have fainted for a second because when I raised my head off the steering wheel my hands were by my side and my driving gloves were off. I sat there for a few minutes until I collected myself. I could smell the ozone in the air.

My head felt like it had living things moving around in it. A strange feeling surged through my body. I looked at myself in the mirror and my hair was standing straight up. It was waving back and forward as if in a breeze.

I thought how insignificant we are when Mother Nature has her way. She wins. But at least for now, I was still alive.

I glanced out my side window. I could just see the side of the mountain. I noticed a trickle of mud coming towards me and it looked like it was gathering speed. I had to get out of here. I managed to start moving again.

I hadn't gone a mile or so when another clap of thunder lifted my car. Lightning struck a tree behind me and fell smouldering across the road. The air felt like it was pure electricity. I was in hell and there wasn't anybody there to help me.

I was terrified but I had to keep moving. When the third clap of thunder struck I thought I was going to die.

The lightening illuminated everything around me and struck a tree to the right of me and caught fire. I could feel the displaced air rock the car as the tree literally exploded. The air was now filled with an acrid smell of burning wood.

The noise of the rain and the thunder was deafening and my ears where hurting so badly I thought I was going to be sick. It was no use, I had to move. I slowly inched my way along. At this rate I wouldn't get to Georges' shop till after one o'clock.

I must only have about five miles left to go, I thought, but I had no point of reference. My body was leaning over the steering wheel trying desperately to see where I was going. My eyes hurt. I rubbed them as I searched for a path through the rain. As I peered through my windshield I could see light ahead of me. It was like looking at a light through a really dark curtain.

As I got closer to the light, and through the mountain, the rain stopped. It stopped as fast as it started and I could feel a huge change in pressure.

Tea, Love & Suspicion

I looked in my rear view mirror and the sky was clear. There were no dark clouds, no rain, how could that be? It was as if I had been the star in a science fiction movie and somebody said, "Cut and print." Back to reality.

Now that I could see, I realized I was only about four miles from the shop.

My right leg was still shaking so badly I could hardly press the gas pedal. It shouldn't take me long to get to the shop, I thought, so I persevered. I couldn't wait to get out of my car. My knuckles were white as I gripped the steering wheel like it was my connection to the ground. I felt that if I let go, I would fall apart.

CHAPTER THREE

I pulled into George's garage and stopped.

My right leg was still shaking and I couldn't release my hands from the steering wheel. George took one look at me and opened my door. "What's wrong Angela, are you ill?" I couldn't speak. He tried to pry my fingers off the wheel. It was if they had become part of the car. When he did manage to get me out, I couldn't stand up. He helped me into his office and sat me on the sofa.

"I'm going to call the doctor." he said. "No George." I managed to say. "Just let me sit a while. A glass of water would be fine." "I'll do better, he said, I'll make you some hot tea." George knew me too well. I just nodded.

I managed to hold the cup of tea and remarkably after only a few minutes I was beginning to feel human again. When I told George what had happened, he was stunned. He thought he had heard thunder but had no idea it was so severe, he hadn't seen a drop of rain. I'm sure he thought I was exaggerating.

George looked at me. "Let's see if they have anything to say on the radio." He turned the radio on just as the news was coming on. "George, did he say the three o'clock news?" "Yes, I was already a little concerned about you when you didn't get here by noon but I thought maybe you had forgotten or you got busy at the office. I was planning on calling you."

We both listened to the radio expecting to hear of this devastating storm. The newscaster mentioned that there was a heavy rain mass had passed quickly though just North of Jenna and the road crews were out checking for flooding. That was it, no big deal. Except I knew it was a big deal and it didn't pass quickly either.

"How could it possibly take me 4 hours to get here George? I could walk it in less time." "I don't know, he said, did you stop somewhere?" I had to think. "Only for a couple of minutes." I said. "I remember saying a little prayer but that couldn't have been more than 5 minutes max." I was only about six miles from here when the storm hit."

"I better check your car." George said as he walked into the shop. "Then I'll get busy and change those tires for you. That should make you feel better."

I sat drinking my tea watching as George put my car up on the hoist. "I just want to check underneath to make sure everything is okay." he said. "The undercarriage looks good no scrapes or dents but what the heck is going on?" he said as I watched him turn each wheel.

He rubbed his head and stared at me. "All four of your rims are so badly bent I'm surprised you made it here. I can't see any other damage. The front end is tight it doesn't seem like anything else is out of place but you must have hit that pavement really hard, twice." Did it not seem weird driving after the storm finished?" he asked. "To tell the truth George, I really don't remember."

He wandered around my car. "Not even a scratch on your car but your tires and wheels are toast." He looked at me and shook his head. "I've never seen anything like this before. It's one for the record books." I think maybe now he was starting to believe me.

"I'll take it for a test run once I get your new wheels on and see if I detect any other problems. As he took off my old wheels and put my new ones on I felt as if my car had been reborn. My nice new BMW was whole again.

He took it for a test run. When he got back he was smiling. "Runs like a new car, he said, I couldn't feel or see any problems, so it's good to go." It made me feel so much better knowing that George had checked it out. George was a fantastic mechanic, everybody said so. I knew my car would be safe to drive home. As we looked at my old discarded tires spread out on the shop floor, George turned to me. "I'm going to keep your wheels here till you make your insurance claim. There's not enough room in your trunk for your spare and your old wheels anyway. In fact, I think I might put these wheels on display and let people guess how they came to look like this."

I was watching George as he put his hands on his hips and shook his head. He slowly turned to me. "Are you still going to have time to visit with my parents while you're down here? They were really looking forward to seeing you, it's been a while." "No." I said. "I'm a little later than I planned on and by the time I take the back road home it should be getting late. I'll just give your mother a quick call to say hello and find out how the roads are out her way."

The route I planned to take was only a couple of miles from their farm. The roads were just fine she said. What rain? I told her we should get together next week.

George had been my late husbands' best friend. Both his parents and mine had come over from Germany the same year so we were very close growing up but, like most people, we didn't see each other as often as we should and I always felt guilty for not keeping in touch more often.

As I hung up the phone and went back into the shop George was still looking a little perplexed as he bent over to get a closer look at the wheels. His obvious concern was starting to worry me; he couldn't take his eyes off my wheels. He heard me come back into the shop and turned to talk to me. "Are you sure you'll be okay Angela? You could always stay at the house if you want." "No, I want to get home before it gets dark so I'm off and running." It was almost 4:30.

I didn't want him to know it but I was still a little shaky. "Besides, don't you have a hockey game to go to tonight George? Your boys will be waiting for you, you better get moving." As I stood up George came over to make sure I could still stand and gave me a lasting hug. "Please." He said with this worried look on his face. "Take it easy, try to get here more often, we all miss you. If you have any problems, call me." "Will do." I said as I drove out of the shop.

I knew the back road so well. It had been our main road for so many years until they made a short cut through the mountain. The road was really a mess but quite navigable. Nobody else was on the road so I was making really good time. It seemed like the same pot holes had been there forever but because few people, other than farmers, used it, it just never got fixed. I had just passed the big plant onto the last stretch of the road to the highway when the unthinkable happened.

CHAPTER FOUR

Damn! It couldn't be a flat tire I just had them put on an hour ago. Yup, it's a flat tire. I know better than to use the back roads but the freeway was sure to be blocked and the traffic would be backed up for miles. Now what? Maybe the Automobile Association would be able to get here? Well that was no help. At least my cell phone works but a three hour wait? I guess our small community isn't ready for disasters. Cab, yes it's ringing and ringing and ringing.

As I sat wondering what to do next I thought about changing it myself but I really wasn't dressed for it. I had only had the car for a couple of months and really wasn't sure what to do. My other car was easy. I had had it for years and knew every nook and cranny.

As I looked in my rear view mirror I saw a figure walking towards me. As he got closer I noticed he was really well dressed, not your typical wanderer but I locked my doors and put my windows up just in case. He knocked on my window. I slowly let the window down a few inches and all I saw were two of the most beautiful green eyes just inches away from me.

"Are you okay?" he said. "Can I help?" He looked at my back tire. "You definitely have a flat tire. Looks like metal sticking out of the sidewall, too bad that looks like a new tire." "Yes." I said as I rolled down the window and looked into the face of an Adonis.

Tea, Love & Suspicion   **11**

He was tanned which made his eyes even more striking. When he smiled he showed the most perfect teeth. He must be the most handsome man I had ever seen. I just sat there for a moment and eventually collected myself. As I got out of the car I noticed the Burberry scarf, the black Pea Jacket and shoes that were not really meant for walking. "I just had these tires put on an hour ago, I said, "and here I sit. I couldn't ask you to change my tire; you're not exactly dressed for getting dirty either." I said. He looked into my eyes. "No problem, at least your tires are new, just pop the trunk." he said in a commanding but friendly manner. It took him no time at all and once more my beautiful BMW was ready to roll.

Of course I offered him a ride, how could I not. I would have been stuck there for hours if he hadn't come along. He leaned back in the seat and took off his toque. Well. He was as bald as a billiard ball and even more handsome than before, if that was possible. I remember thinking how perfect the shape of his head was. He was young, maybe 10-12 years younger than me but it was hard to tell. As he buckled up his seat belt he introduced himself as Frank Winston. He had just arrived into town yesterday and would be working at the plant down the road. Apparently his car was supposed to be delivered last night but there was so much flooding in the area there was a delay and it was arriving tomorrow. "And who may I ask are you?" he said. It took me a moment to reply. "I'm sorry, my name is Angela Bremner and I live about 15 minutes from here although I have a feeling it will take much longer tonight."

CHAPTER FIVE

He said he was staying at the Wycliff Hotel. It was the best hotel in over 100 miles and was built in the 20's. It had all the wonderful things that made a hotel a destination. It had brass, copper, stained glass windows and beautifully carved oak wood. It also had the best restaurant I have ever been in and I have travelled through at least 15 countries. "That's a really nice hotel, you'll like it." I said.

It must have taken more than an hour to reach his hotel and we had been chatting all the way, he was so easy to talk to. As we pulled up to his hotel it was almost 7 o'clock. "Please, join me for dinner," he said. "I'm starving and I'm sure you are too." I couldn't believe it, I said yes so quickly I didn't even think twice. Maybe I was more hungry than I thought. The meal was to die for as per usual and as we sat drinking our wine I looked at my watch for the first time since we sat down. It was 10 o'clock and we hadn't stopped talking.

"We'll have to do this again," he said as he walked me to my car. We had exchanged phone numbers. I thought that if he didn't know anyone else he might eventually call me which would be nice. I had enjoyed his company. Just as I was about to get into my car he gave me a hug and kissed me gently on the mouth.

I've been a widow for almost 14 years and I've always been fast enough to divert a kiss from the mouth to the cheek and

Tea, Love & Suspicion

many had tried. I really didn't see this one coming but strangely enough it wasn't offensive at all. A first for me in many many years. "Thank you so much for saving me from an incredibly long walk and for the wonderful company." He said. "Well," I said, "we wouldn't be here if you hadn't changed my tire." I waved good-by and set off home. I could still feel his kiss.

CHAPTER SIX

I was glad it was Friday, I felt like sleeping late.

The doorbell rang and Margaret was standing looking a little upset. "What's wrong," I said. She told me to put the kettle on and we could discuss it. I'd known Margaret for over 20 years. I used to work part time for the same company as she did and we became fast friends. She was actually old enough to be my mother but she was the best friend I ever had. Her husband had passed away 2 years before my husband and the bond we had was one few people ever have. We never had a wrong word or even a disagreement in all those years. "Okay," she said, "who the hell is the man in your life?" "What," I said. "How, I mean what have you heard?"

"Well." she said. "I heard he was the most handsome man and should be on some magazine cover, he's tall and he kissed you goodnight. You don't think I drove over here just to have some tea do you?" I told her how we had met and that he seemed like a really nice man. "You should be more careful Angela, she said, he could be a murderer or something." I looked at her and frowned. "I know we live in a small town Margaret but who the heck woke you up to tell you the latest gossip on my so called love life?" "Oh, it was Gail. I guess you were too busy to notice Bert and Gail; they were celebrating their 40th anniversary at the hotel and couldn't wait to tell me. Gail was really surprised to see you their but jealous when she saw who you were with.

"Better looking than Brad Pitt." she said. "Okay Angela, what's his name? How old is he? What does he do for a living? Is he married? Come on Angela tell me everything."

I could only tell her his name and that he started working at the Plant on Morgan Road and that his car should be arriving today. We finished our tea and although Margaret wasn't sure I'd told her everything, she knew I was pretty level headed and just gave me a lecture on picking up strange men. She had just finished her lecture when the phone rang. It was Frank. I could feel my face flush and Margaret gave me the evil eye. "Sure Frank that sounds fine, my address is 562 West Road, 45 minutes would be great." As I hung up the phone Margaret was waiting for the details. "Well, he just got his car and wants me to show him around, he'll be here in 45 minutes, just time for me to have a shower and get ready."

Margaret got up and was on her way to the door. "Don't leave yet Marg. I would like you to meet him. Have another cup of tea while I get dressed." 44 minutes later the doorbell rang and I opened the door. I wasn't sure if I had just been dreaming about Frank or if he really was as good as I remembered. He most definitely was.

"This is my good friend Margaret, Margaret. Frank, Frank, Margaret." "I'm so glad to meet you." He said as he shook Margaret's hand. I could see that Margaret was for once, lost for words. "Well you two, I must get moving so I will talk to you later, wont I Angela?" "Yes, you will." I said.

I almost bumped into her as she stopped in her tracks in the doorway. "What the hell is that?" Marg. said. "It looks like something from outer space." "I guess, it must be Franks'." I said. Frank was standing right behind me. "Yes," he said, "it just arrived this morning. It's a pro-to type were working on." "Oh." Marg. said. "Call me later Angela." She hadn't been feeling well lately so I would have called her anyway.

I grabbed my coat and purse and walked out to the car and stood at the passenger door looking for the door handle, it didn't have one. The door opened by itself as Frank stood by my side. I just looked at him and didn't say a word. "It's Okay." he said. "It doesn't bite." As I sat down the safety harness automatically adjusted itself and locked, it made me nervous.

As we drove off I was beginning to wonder what planet Frank was from. The dash board was like something you would see in a plane, too much for me to understand. It was odd that as soon as we drove down the street and we started talking, everything seemed strangely normal. Why was it that I felt so comfortable and trusting with this man that I really didn't know? We drove for miles and although this was now a small community it had a lot of history from days gone by.

We stopped off at the farmers market and picked up lots of fresh fruit, vegetables and some fish that had just been caught the previous night. I said it was my turn to make dinner. Frank was all for it. "A home cooked meal would be terrific." he said. I wasn't too sure. It had been a long time since I had entertained a man in my home.

CHAPTER SEVEN

We got back to the house around 3:30. "How about a coffee?" I said. I had noticed at the restaurant he seemed to like the special type coffee. "I only have the regular type, I'm a tea drinker myself but I do have de-cafe or regular." "I'll have tea if you don't mind. Just the regular tea would be fine." He smiled. As we sat drinking our tea I thought I better give Margaret a call before she called me.

I went into my bedroom so I could answer what I knew would be personal questions. She had so many questions and unfortunately I had few answers. "Margaret, you know me," I said, "I wouldn't entertain a person who I didn't think was a decent human being and he is not staying the night." I think she was relieved. "Actually for as much as I just met him for a couple of minutes." Margaret said. "I really did like him, he has a calmness about him and obviously you like him Angela, that's what I care about." "I know," I said, "don't worry I really will be fine and I must admit, it's nice to have the company." "Okay kiddo, be good. I'll talk to you on Wednesday. I have a Doctors' appointment on Monday." "Did you want me to take you in Marg.? I can take Monday off, it's no problem." I said. Of course she didn't want me to but I was always concerned for her.

Frank and I had the most wonderful dinner. It doesn't happen all the time but every once in a while things turn out perfectly and this was that time. Trouble is, now he thinks I'm a really good cook and I'm only a sometimes good cook without too much imagination.

I had eaten more than I should and suggested we relax in the living room. As we walked into the living room I wondered what kind of movies he liked, what music he liked. I had lots of movies on DVD and he was all for taking it easy tonight. He chose the movie. I know he would have probably chosen something different if he were on his own, probably something my son Jessie would like. We settled for Raiders of the Lost Arc, one of my favourites. I had only seen it once before and that was years ago. After the movie was over he said that he had an early meeting the next day, so he left around 9:30.

It seemed strange to have a meeting on Sunday but he had only just arrived in town so I was sure he had lots to catch up on. After all, he had spent the whole day with me. As he left he turned to face me. He looked straight into my eyes, thanked me for a wonderful day, gave me a hug and the most gentle kiss. He had the softest lips. I could feel my knees go weak. "Is it okay to call you tomorrow?" he said. I'm sure his knees were in great shape but I was feeling uncomfortable and casually leaned against the doorway. I hoped that if the time came for me to say no, I could, but this wasn't one of those times. "Any time." I said. As I closed the door I had to tell myself that what I really needed from him was his companionship. He was too young and too handsome and although I felt great when I was with him, I didn't want to get hurt, and I had the feeling that one day I would. I wondered if I should really stop this before I got too attached to him. Was I really making too much out of this? I had only known him for a couple of days why not just relax and enjoy his company. I could handle it. All I had to do was remind myself that he was only 10 years older than my son and hopefully, my maternal instincts would save me.

CHAPTER EIGHT

As I woke up the next morning and stretched, I felt unusually happy. I was always in a good mood but for the first time in years I had actually been out on a date with someone I actually liked being with. Enough of that I said to myself I need breakfast.

Once I had eaten I felt energetic and decided to take a look downstairs. My son Jessie had always wanted his own space and he was coming home on break in a couple of months. His room on the main floor was huge but he always liked the thoughts of having his own place where he could have his friends over.

I had really missed Jessie since he left for Med. school. He was one of the lucky ones. When his father passed away he had left a substantial amount for Jessie's education. He wanted to be a doctor for as long as I remember and he was living his well-deserved dream. He always took extra courses and although he was what some call a nerd; he had a goal and was determined to reach it. He had the best sense of humour of anyone I knew and he was a joy to have around, and I missed him terribly.

As I looked around the rooms it looked like it would work out perfectly. I should have converted this years ago. It was filled with memories. Games and unused exercise equipment. Table tennis, shuffle board, darts and every board game you could imagine. When my husband John was alive we spent hours down here with Jessie. Those were the good days. I loved my life.

John and I had started up our own business when computer programming was in its early stages and we were making a very comfortable living. We had built our house shortly after we came back from England and our home looked like it belonged in the English countryside but with central heating. We loved bay windows, fireplaces, high ceilings, picture rails, separate toilets and circular drive ways. We had 4 fireplaces in our home and John and I had spent time enjoying each one. Everybody loved John. He was the kind of person you wanted to know. He was fun, handsome and very intelligent. I fell in love with him when I was 14. We were married when I turned 17 and he was 20. It was the perfect marriage for 7 years. We were successful both professionally and personally.

John's heart attack was something that still affected me. How could someone so young die so quickly? He had just been given a clean bill of health 6 months before. It felt so unfair. The truth was that I still loved him. He had been gone now for almost 14 years but somehow he was alive in this room. I know he would be upset with me for dwelling on the past but how could I not when there were so many memories scattered around me. Suddenly I felt very sad and the tears were streaming down my face. It was almost too hard to bear so I took one more look around. It was time.

On my way upstairs I knew I had to call Jack my friendly contractor. It would be a wonderful surprise for Jessie and I knew that John would approve.

As I walked into the kitchen, I suddenly had the urge to clean. I started in the kitchen and worked my way through the house. I think it must have been therapeutic, because I was hungry. It was almost 3 o'clock and I hadn't even stopped for lunch. An egg sandwich and a cup of tea. That should get me through till dinner time. I just sat down to eat lunch when the phone rang. It was Frank. "I've been up to my ears in meetings

Tea, Love & Suspicion   **21**

today," he said, I just had to take a break and hear your cheerful voice." It was a good thing he hadn't called a few hours ago, I wouldn't have been so cheerful. I think I had just exhausted myself and it had helped get rid of the sadness that plagued me periodically. Only Margaret saw that side of me.

"I was wondering Angela, would you like to go out tomorrow night for dinner and a movie? It will give me something to look forward to. Also, before I forget, I was wondering if you could help me look for a place to live. I really like the Hotel but it looks like I will be here for some time. Something clean and comfortable. The price doesn't matter but it would have to have a lot of charm. Maybe we could talk about that over dinner, if you don't mind?" "Sure," I said, "I would be glad to."

I told him I had a friend in the business. "I could ask her and she could line up whatever was available, how does that sound?" "That sounds great Angela, thank you. So I'll pick you up at 6 o'clock if that's alright?" "Sounds good," I said. "See you tomorrow Frank." As I hung up the phone I dived into my lunch, I was starving. After I ate I felt so much more relaxed and started to day dream of a nice luxurious bubble bath, a nice warm fire and a good book. My plans for the evening made me feel like myself again. I only had a shower in my en-suite so a bath in the main bathroom felt like a day at the spa. I always lit the candles and played my favourite music. I should do that more often I thought to myself, it's been a long time since I had pampered myself.

CHAPTER NINE

As I arrived at the office the next morning I looked around and realized just how much our little company had grown. Most of my staff had been with us since John and I started up the business. We pretty well started up the way we intended to finish. Every employee had shares in the company. We had the best medical benefits and each year, depending on how many years they had been with us, they got a healthy bonus. We even had second generation staff with us now. Some of the young ones were giving us a challenge. Their computer skills were important for us to grow and they had a built in loyalty for the company. They were family. I think that part of the reason we had become so successful was that we were a small company and could adapt more quickly to the sudden changes that happened regularly in this business.

Mary was the overall manager and my friend. She was a couple of years older than I and pretty well ran the business when I was away. She had my total trust. Mary came into my office with a cup of tea. I kept telling her, year after year that she didn't have to do that but she didn't listen. We would always take the first 30 minutes of the day just chit chatting. Then we got down to business. She always asked how my weekends were but today she had a smile on her face. I think everyone was wondering who Frank was, so I filled her in on what we had been doing and how I had met him. "Lucky you." She said.

"He sounds too good to be true and that car of his is something else. When Fred came home the other night he had seen it in town and couldn't stop talking about it. When I asked him what the driver looked like he said he hadn't even noticed. Typical man." "Don't worry, you'll get to meet him," I said, "he's really quite sociable and it seems like he might be staying around for a while." The phone rang and it was back to business.

I gave a quick call to Jean and asked her to look for what was available to rent in the real estate business and asked her to e-mail anything that sounded worthwhile. Real Estate wasn't exactly the best business to be in right now, people were pretty much staying put and I hadn't noticed too many for rent signs lately. Oh well, I knew Jean would do her best.

CHAPTER TEN

The rule of the office was that at 4:30 we closed the office and we all went home, unless there was an emergency. Most of the staff had families still at home and John and I always thought that family time was important. It worked out well for me too. On the way out I grabbed the e-mail that Jean had sent and didn't even look at it. I figured I could go over it with Frank at dinner and see if there might be something interesting. Dinner and a movie sounded great and I was really looking forward to it.

It was amazing. Frank must drive around the block to make sure he was right on time. 6 o'clock on the dot and the doorbell rang. "Do you mind?" he said. "I would like to use the little boys' room." "It's the Lou just on the landing." I said, as he kissed me on the cheek and hurried past me. "No! No! Not the bathroom." I said. "The small door on the right." "Okay", he said, "I got it." He came out of the Lou and went into to bathroom to wash his hands. He was laughing as he came towards me. He gave me a big hug and lifted me off my feet. He could hardly talk for laughing. "I found the bathroom the other night. I saw the bathtub, the sink and that was all. I must admit, now I know where the Lou is, I won't leave so early next time. What on earth made you put a pull toilet in your home?" I thought it was a linen closet. "Well." I said, "John and I had just got back from England when we built our house and we just loved

Tea, Love & Suspicion

the idea. Besides, I hardly ever use it, I have my own." We both laughed. He wasn't the first nor would he be the last to fall prey to "The Lou". Maybe I should get a sign for it.

CHAPTER ELEVEN

Frank was still smiling as we drove to the Hotel. The doorman greeted Frank. "Good evening Mr. Winston." He gave me a smile and a nod. I gather it was impolite to call the lady by her name because I had known Tom for years. We were even in the same class in high school. The Wycliff was nothing, if not discreet and I thought it was a good part of the hotel's charm.

We had a wonderful dinner as usual and looked over the e-mail that Jean had sent. "Nothing much." I said. "One of them might be interesting but the other two are really not in a good area and they are a little out of town. If you want to have a look at the one on Victoria Street, you can give Jean a call, she's really nice and would be glad to see if there might be something else you would be interested in. Her number is on the sheet." He folded the paper and put it in his pocket and signed for the bill. "Do you mind if I go to my room?" he said, "I would like to change into something more comfortable and maybe we could walk to the theatre. It would be good to stretch my legs, I've been sitting much too much lately." "I know what you mean," I said, "I feel the same way. I haven't eaten so well for years and it's beginning to show."

It was only a few blocks to the theatre but the walk felt good. As we left the hotel he reached out for my hand. Maybe that would seem quite normal to someone else but I felt really strange. I'm sure he felt my moment of hesitation. I think the last time I held hands with anyone other than Jessie was John. Somehow it felt more sensual and personal with Frank. As we walked towards the theatre I felt my body relax and noticed that people were looking at us. If I do say so myself, we really were a handsome couple. Frank was 6'2" and had an athletic body. I was only 5'6" and felt tiny beside him. I hadn't really thought much about the difference in our height. I guess most of the time we were sitting so I hadn't noticed till now. I liked it; it made me feel safe in his company and the warmth of my hand in his felt good.

We were just getting to our seats when I noticed Gail and Bert a few rows ahead of us. Damn, I hoped I could get to talk to Margaret before Gail spread the word, although, I think Gail's gossip was telepathic and phones came in a close second. Fortunately, the movie was great. There wasn't too much blood and gore and it had lots of humour in it which made the 2 hours pass very quickly. However, there was no escaping Gail on the way out. I think she must have been on a track team in a previous life. I introduced Frank to Gail and Bert who came puffing along behind her. I certainly wasn't embarrassed to be with Frank but this was a new experience for me. Gail and Bert were very gracious and didn't linger. They walked left and we turned right. Frank held my hand again as we walked back to the hotel.

By the time he drove me home it was almost 10 o'clock. As we stood in the doorway I asked if he would like a night cap. "I have a wine you might like," I said, "my coffee is bad but you're welcome to suffer through it if you're brave enough." "Sure," he said, "just a short drink, I have another early meeting tomorrow and I still have to go over my notes." He only stayed a short while. As we stood in the doorway he held my face in his hands and kissed me. Still that gentle kiss, but this time it was different. It was more than a brotherly kiss but less than a lover.

I could feel my whole body respond but backed up just enough to look him in the eyes. I don't know what I expected to see, but his eyes were smiling. I got the feeling that he was enjoying this cat and mouse game. I just couldn't figure out who was the cat. "I'll call you, or you call me," he said, "any way we'll be in touch tomorrow, won't we?" "Sure we will and thank you," I said, "I had a great time tonight. And, by the way, I don't know if you noticed or not but I think all the gossipers were in the theatre tonight, so stay tuned." "Not to worry," he said, "I have thick skin." With that he was gone and part of me was wishing he had stayed a little longer and the other part of me was on her way to bed, dog tired. Oh boy, I thought, I better remember to call Margaret first thing in the morning, it was too late now. I had planned on calling her anyway to find out what the doctor had to say.

CHAPTER TWELVE

I got up early and my first thought was of Margaret. I better call her before anyone else did, but there was no answer. That was odd. Maybe she decided to sleep in today and turned her phone off. She did that sometimes but I always worried about her. I decided to call her once I got to the office.

I had no sooner walked into the office when the whole office started to clap. "Oh No.!" I said. "The gossipers have already struck. Okay you guys, I really don't need an ovation, a bow would do." The whole crew had heard about the hand holding and our trip to the theatre. "Is *nothing* sacred?" I said. Actually I think that they were just really happy that I had found someone to take me out of my what they thought was a celibate life. Little did they know. It was still celibate.

Mary came into my office, it was almost lunch time. I was on the phone trying to reach Margaret. "I don't understand why Margaret isn't answering her phone Mary," I said, "now I'm getting a little concerned." "She probably forgot to turn it back on", Mary said, "why don't you go over there. We're pretty quiet in the office right now and I know you, you'll do nothing but worry." "Yes," I said, "I better otherwise I won't be able to concentrate anyway."

As I drove over to Marg.'s townhouse I kept thinking of what I would do without her. We had been so close for so many years. I knew she was getting on in years but the thought of her getting sick hadn't really crossed my mind. I guess we just feel that everyone we care about lasts forever and sometimes they don't. I knocked on her door and still no answer. I had always had a key to her place because I looked after things when she went out of town, so I let myself in.

Everything was neat and tidy. Nothing was out of place and it looked like she hadn't been there last night either. I felt the kettle to see if it might be warm but it wasn't. Now I was really worried. I decided to phone the hospital, just in case. "I'm calling to see if you have a Margaret Brown registered." I said. It seemed like forever before the operator said. "Yes, we have a Margaret Brown, she's in room 210." Obviously they wouldn't give me any details so I drove like a mad woman over to the hospital.

Margaret had always been immaculate, never a hair out of place and her clothing was perfectly colour co-ordinated, but when I looked inside her room it seemed like there was another person there. That person looked about 15 years older, but it was Margaret. As I walked toward her she opened her eyes. "What the hell are you doing here?" she said. "I've come for a visit and a cup of tea, what else?" I bent down and hugged her. She seemed so frail all of a sudden. "What happened?" I blurted out. "How come you didn't let me know what was going on? I was sick with worry." "Well Angela, it doesn't look good. I had a bad turn yesterday and they feel I am not a good candidate for an operation. My heart has been a problem for a while now and I think they are going to keep me in here for a few days to see if some medication will help."

"Is there anything you need?" I asked, fighting back the tears. "Yes, bring me that man of yours. That should get my heart started again." I couldn't help it, I laughed until I cried. Her sense of humour didn't let her down, even now. "I was thinking more like a nice nightgown and matching panties." I said.

"Well, if that's all you can do I'll have to settle for that. Bring my toothbrush my hairbrush as well." She said. "No problem." I said. "I don't have to work today so I'll be back in half an hour. Anything else?" "Well." She said slowly. "You know you're the executrix of my estate and I need you to take care of things for me if anything happens." I felt sick. "Marg., don't talk like that." I said. "Please, you're going to get better and then we can talk about it." "No." she said, "I just want you to know a few things, just in case."

She was speaking slowly. "You know my freezer has more than meat in it don't you? Well, leave the meat and take the rest of the stuff in there and that's an order. Also, you will find my Will in the side table beside my bed. There's a letter for you in there too, just in case." "I think I've heard one too many just in cases Marg." I said. "Well, you get going and don't forget my tooth paste; the stuff in here is terrible." "You know I love you, don't you Marg.? You are my most special friend and I don't know what I would do without you." "Angela, the feeling is mutual." she said, with tears in her eyes. "You have meant so much to me over the years. You have been my daughter by choice and I thank you for all the years you have been my closest friend. Now get out of here, I need my nice nighty."

As I was walking out of the room I just about ran into an old friend. We had gone through school together. For years we had played on the same tennis team. "Terry, how are you?" I said, "I haven't seen you for years." "Oh my goodness, it's good to see you again Angela." she said. "It's been a long time. I'm sure you must have heard I went to work in the city hospital after I got my RN. I only decided to come home when my mother became ill." She said. "Are you a friend of Margaret's?" "The best." I said. "I'm so worried about her." Terry grabbed my hand. "I'll keep an eye on her for you. Will you be coming back later?" "Yes," I said, "I should only be gone for the time it takes me to pick up a few of her things. Thank you so much Terry, see you later. We'll have to keep in touch now that you're back in town."

I rushed over to Marg.'s house and walked into her bedroom. I couldn't help but notice that on top of the nightstand was a collage of pictures of her niece Gail. She never had children of her own so when Gail's parents passed away they became very close. I didn't have time to reminisce. I looked in the nightstand and there was her Will and a letter, addressed to me. I put the letter in my pocket and looked for her prettiest nightgown and of course she did have matching underwear. I think she made them herself. Her toothbrush and toothpaste looked like she had laid them out especially for me to find. I didn't bother with the freezer as I wanted to get back to the hospital as soon as possible. I was so glad we didn't have a big police force because I was definitely speeding.

As I walked into the hospital Terry was standing beside the customer service counter. When our eyes met, I knew there was a problem. She pulled me to one side and asked me to have a seat. I knew it wasn't good news. "I'm so sorry Angela, I'm afraid I have some bad news for you."

I don't remember exactly what she said, my brain just froze. When I eventually could hear what she was saying I realized that Margaret had passed away just moments after I left. Terry had been with her holding her hand and her last words were of me. That was it, I thought I was going to have a heart attack. Terry brought me some water and some Kleenex and I was at a loss of what to do now. I don't know how long I sat there, half the time I was crying and the rest of the time I just stared into space. I knew I had to pull myself together.

I phoned the office and talked to Mary. All of my staff knew Margaret; she had been to all our outings since day one with John and me. She was always the life of the party. I could still hear her laughter. Mary was probably the closest to her and

Tea, Love & Suspicion

I knew she was suffering with me. It was 3 o'clock and I told her to close the office and go home. I would see her tomorrow and maybe she could help me with the arrangements that I was going to have to make. Regardless of our grief. I knew Mary was crying but she was always so supportive and she didn't let me down. "Don't worry Angela, we can go over what needs to be done tomorrow." she said. "Oh, by the way, Frank phoned and asked you to call him." "I will, I said, thank you." I guess I had my cell phone off while I was at the hospital because he never usually called me at the office.

I wasn't sure what to tell Frank or that I could even talk but I phoned him anyway. As I told him what had happened he was noticeably upset too. "I am so sorry," he said. "I had a feeling that something wasn't right when you didn't answer your phone. I didn't really know her," he said, but it was obvious that she cared a great deal for you and I am so sorry for your loss. Is there anything I can do for you?" It was obvious that I was crying. "Would it help if I came over tonight?" He said. "I would like that Frank," I said, "I really don't want to be alone but I doubt I will be good company." "I don't mind." He said. "I know what you are going through. I can be there around 5:30, would that be a good time?" "Yes, that would be good. Thank you Frank." I said. "See you then."

CHAPTER THIRTEEN

5:30 on the dot the door-bell rang, it was Frank. I must have looked like hell, but I really didn't care. I just stood in the doorway. He stood there for a second and then just held me and didn't let go until I relaxed. We walked into the living room and sat down. Frank put his arm around me and consoled me until I fell asleep. I don't know how long I slept but I woke up with my head in Franks lap. Poor man, I don't think he had been able to move. As I managed to come too Frank stretched and stood up. He said the magic words. "How about a cup of tea?" He asked me if I was hungry. I really wasn't but I knew he must be. "How about a Pizza," I said. "I guess we should eat something." We decided to order Pesto Pizza, thin crust. I had already found out we were both allergic to peppers. I never could understand why they always seemed to put peppers, green, red or yellow on or in pretty well everything. We sat and ate our Pizza and I think we both decided that Pizza would be our last choice next time. Frank stayed until 10:00 and I suggested he go home and get some sleep. As he was leaving he held me and kissed me on the cheek. "If I can help at all," he said, "please just let me know." I cried myself to sleep.

Mary, Gail and I worked on the eulogy the next morning and put it in the local paper. News had travelled very quickly throughout the town and I had spent most of the day on the phone. I had made an evening appointment with Marg.'s lawyer

Tea, Love & Suspicion

to go over the details of her Will and to arrange for her funeral. It was a very simple will. She left everything to her niece Gail and some personal things to me. She knew I had enough money and had provided some cash in her freezer to more than take care of her funeral. However, also in her Will I found out the she had spelled out in no uncertain terms that she should be cremated and have a party at my place on the first weekend following her death. So she kept her sense of humour to the end. She knew I worked better under pressure. Thank goodness for Mary, I couldn't have done it without her and our staff. Gail pitched in where she could even though she was almost inconsolable in her grief.

We didn't know how many people would come to the tribute so we had a caterer supply the food. It was an unbelievable turn out. People who lived here but I hadn't seen for years showed up to honour Margaret. Frank was by my side just about all day and had now been introduced to pretty well the whole of our small town. He really was a surprise. He looked very comfortable no matter who had cornered him. We had so many people wanting to say their piece we didn't see the last guest leave until 7 o'clock. I was exhausted. Frank put the kettle on and ordered me to sit and I was more than willing. After we had our tea Frank suggested that he leave and come back tomorrow to take me into the big city for a change of pace. I agreed, I needed to get away.

CHAPTER FOURTEEN

Frank had been looking for a house or townhouse to rent but so far he had had no luck. I saw a few of them with him and I wasn't very impressed with what was available. He had been looking for the last couple of weeks and was getting a little frustrated. We had just come back to my home when the phone rang. It was Jessie. He was getting a couple of months break and would be coming home. I was so excited. He had been gone for so long and I had a surprise for him.

I had had the lower level converted into a beautiful suite for Jessie and it looked fantastic, much better than I had imagined. It was expensive but it was worth it. I had also arranged to have some work done on my bathroom but I would do that later on in the month. "Let me know what flight you're coming in on and I'll pick you up," I said. "Great Mom, you're the best." He said. Frank had obviously heard the conversation and wondered if I had told him that I had a new friend. I told him that I had but really, I hadn't. Now that Jessie had confirmed that he was coming home maybe I would tell him next week when I talked to him. A little white lie but I didn't know how he would accept me having a man in my life. I was sure he would be really supportive but somehow I felt guilty.

Frank and I had been spending almost every evening together and our parting was always the same. The hugs were getting stronger and the kisses were getting longer. We snuggled when we watched TV and held hands. I was beginning to wonder. He had never made any further advances and although that was just fine with me, we were both young healthy people. I had a sudden thought. Maybe he was gay. Oh well, I thought, who cares, I felt lucky that I had him in my life and didn't want to lose his friendship. It was at this point that I suggested that he consider moving into my spare room. We spent most of our time together anyway. "Come on Frank, take a look and see what you think." I said. I took him into what was Jessie's room and he was really surprised. "This is huge!" he said. "A fireplace in the bedroom, a walk in closet a big bay window and a study area but no en-suite, just the Lou and the main bathroom. Not to worry, I'm beginning to like that Lou anyway."

"It's really fantastic." He said. "Do you really think that Jessie would be fine with this arrangement?" "Of course he would." I said. "He's going to be so happy with his own suite and I know you two would really get along. We can play it by ear if you want; you don't have to sign a lease or anything." "Well," he said, "I must admit, this is the best place I have seen so far. Of course we would have to find a way for me to pay my way. I could pay for all of the utilities, the gardener and any repairs you feel you need and I promise to keep taking you out to dinner, or whatever you want would be fine with me."

I didn't have a mortgage so I really wasn't sure what would be appropriate either but his suggestions sounded fair. "Well Frank, it's up to you when you want to move in. Weren't you going out of town next week?" I said. "Yes," he said, "I'll be leaving Monday and back on Thursday. How about I move out of the hotel on Saturday would that work for you?" "Sure", I said, "sounds perfect." And that was that. I now had a live in, possibly gay boyfriend. I really didn't know any gay people so I wasn't sure if gays had friendships like ours. I would imagine so but I didn't know anyone that I could ask. It really didn't matter one way or the other, he made me feel happy and had been there for me any time I needed him. I don't know how I would have survived without him when Margaret died. Not only that, we hadn't had an argument or even a heated discussion. Happiness is, I thought. Gay or not.

I was glad Frank was away for a few days, it gave me time to catch up at work and to have some time to myself. I had one of those wonderful spa nights with about 20 candles and lots of bubble bath. I made an appointment to have a massage and I had a pedicure and a manicure, it felt good but I really missed Frank's company. I thought of getting my hair cut but it had taken me so long to grow it I decided not to. I could always put it in a ponytail when it got in my way.

As I sat thinking of all the things I was going to do I realized that I had to let Jessie know what was going on and I really wasn't sure how I was going to tell him. Frank and I had an unusual relationship and I am sure most of people wouldn't believe that we had never made love. I admit I had felt like it but there was always an invisible line drawn and it seemed to be mutual. I picked up the phone and dialled.

Jessie answered on the first ring and surprised me. "Were you sitting on the phone Jessie?" I said. "No Mum," he said, "I just hung up the phone when you called." We chit chatted for a while and then I told him about Frank. To my astonishment he was fine with it. In fact, he was glad that I had found someone to keep me company and that he was looking forward to meeting him. What a relief that was. I didn't tell him that Frank was now living at the house because it would have spoiled the surprise when I showed him his new suite. As far as Jessie knew, we only had a two, if not very large, bedroom house. Jessie always gave up his room and slept down stairs if we had company. If I had told him about our new house guest I would have had to tell him about the new suite I had built for him. I knew he would be happy with whatever I did, so long as I was happy so was he.

CHAPTER FIFTEEN

When Frank got back from his trip I was getting excited to see him again. It had only been 4 days but it felt much longer. As he walked through the door he swept me up in his arms and kissed me like he hadn't seen me for a year. It was obvious, we were definitely glad to see each other although it was much more obvious with him. How wonderful it felt when I knew he wouldn't be leaving. I had made a special dinner for him. He was hungry and he was enjoying every mouthful. As he finished, he leaned back in the chair and gave a big sigh. "That was fantastic, thank you." he said.

"How was your trip?" I asked. "Pretty good, everything seems to be turning out better than I thought, it was good." he said. He never elaborated on his business. I didn't know what he was working on or where he went. I know he went into the city quite often but I felt that business is business and he would tell me more in his own time. I knew the plant he was working in and gather that he was the CEO and that they were involved in advanced electronics. I thought maybe it had something to do with his car, but I was only guessing. He did have that secretive side to him and I was aware that I really didn't know him very well, other than our personal relationship. I often wondered where his family was, who they were and where they were. Now that he was living in my home I felt that those questions would be answered in good time. I guess I had never

Tea, Love & Suspicion   **41**

asked him personal questions either so no wonder I didn't have the answers. However, I had always been a pretty good judge of character and I felt very safe in his company. That was good enough for me, for now.

Jessie was arriving in a couple of days and I was busy making sure that everything was just perfect. Everything was, except for my bathroom. I was having some work done on my en- suite next week. I was hoping that I could have had it done sooner but there were few good contractors and I wanted Jack who had done the work on Jessie's suite. He was a busy man but Jack didn't think it would take too long once he got started and he would try to keep it functional for me while he did the work.

Frank asked me if I wanted him to go with me to pick Jessie up at the airport but I needed time alone with Jessie. I had to break the news about Frank. I still couldn't think of a way to tell him that Frank was now living at the house without spoiling the surprise of his new living quarters.

CHAPTER SIXTEEN

As I looked up at the arrival board, I found out that the flight had already landed. That was great. I hated waiting around the baggage area. As the people started to come towards the carrousel I spotted Jessie right away. We were waving like crazy people. We were a hugger type family and as we hugged each other he told me how wonderful I looked and that he was really glad to be home. He looked older, maybe more masculine I though. My boy had grown into a man. By the time his luggage hit the carousel he had told me all the things he had been missing and there were a few. "I missed you most of all Mum," he said, "but I missed my buddies, especially Barry. He got married." He said. "Did you know that? Not only that", he said, "they have a baby boy, one month old. It doesn't pay to go away, does it?" He always talked so fast like his speech had to keep ahead of his brain. He was so smart but so much fun to be around. I really hadn't got a word in sideways so there was no conversation about Frank.

"I have a great surprise for you when you get home but I can't tell you what it is yet. Actually, I have two surprises for you," I said, "but they will have to wait till we get home." "Oh, come on Mum, that's not fair, you know me I can't stand the suspense." "Just wait." I said. "We're only 5 minutes from the house, be patient." I had got this far so I wasn't going to break. As we drove up to the house I noticed that Franks' car wasn't there. That was a good thing, he probably timed it. If Frank had been sitting at the kitchen table, it might have been awkward.

Jessie was obviously happy to be home and headed up the stairs to his room with his suitcase. "Just wait Jessie," I said, "I have something to show you. Follow me." We headed down to the lower level and opened the door. "What the heck," he said, "this is unbelievable. Is this all mine?" He walked into the room and flung himself across the bed. "Wow Mum you really went all out, look at this, I even have my own bathroom. This is the best but it took you long enough. Maybe I would have stayed home if this had been done a couple of years ago." "Well, I'm glad I didn't," I said, "you were meant to be a doctor." After taking it all in, we wandered upstairs.

"I also have another surprise for you." I said timidly. "You know I mentioned that I had found a new friend, named Frank. Well, I kind of rented your old room to him." I pretty well blurted out the rest. "He's been a great comfort to me especially when Margaret passed away. He looked all over and couldn't find a suitable place to live, so, I thought he could live here and protect me." "Protect you?" Jessie said. "That's a joke. I think he may be the one who needs protection." We both laughed. He knew I was strong willed and quite capable of looking after myself.

Just perfectly timed as usual Frank rang the door-bell, I knew it was him. It was as if he had been listening for just the right moment. As I opened the door he could see Jessie standing behind me so there was no hug or kiss, just a friendly greeting. "Frank, this is my son Jessie." I could see the look on Jessie's face and I knew that Frank was not what he expected him to be. I think he thought he might look more like a homeless man.

Jessie extended his hand and said he was pleased to meet him and Frank said he mentioned that it was obvious that he had been missed. Now what, I thought, maybe a cup of tea would be a good ice breaker, it always was for me.

"How about a nice cup of tea," I said, "let's go to the kitchen." The kitchen was always a good place for comfortable conversation and a cup of tea would sooth my nerves. "Still don't know how to make coffee Mum?" Jessie asked as he looked at Frank. I could see that they both thought I made lousy coffee and they communicated in that one look. After that we let Jessie do the talking, he did it so well. He had been up to his ears studying and really hadn't had time for much of anything else. He had found a study buddy named Joe and they were both acing their tests. Unfortunately Joe had to have a part time job. His mother had raised him on her own and it was his chance to make good. "I respect Joe so much Mum, Jessie said, "he works so hard and he's always so cheerful. I really feel privileged to know him and feel so grateful to Dad for taking care of things for me, I won't let him down."

Jessie stayed home the first night and Frank went to bed early. After Frank said his good nights and went to his room, Jessie just looked at me. "Wow Mum, that's quite a boarder you have there," he said to me. "I was picturing someone quite different. He's pretty young and very good looking. I should introduce him to some of the hot spots in town. I could use him as bait." "Jessie, that's not nice." I said. I know he was only joking but then again, he didn't know just how close Frank and I had become. "He's really a very nice man Jessie and I'm sure he's had his share of hot spots in the city." I said defensively. "I was only joking Mum, really, I think I like him, he's obviously very smart and really likes you."

Well Mum I'm exhausted and I just can't wait to try my new room out. He gave me a goodnight kiss and put his dishes in the sink. "I think we should all have an early night tonight." I said, "We can talk more in the morning." Well, I thought,

Tea, Love & Suspicion 45

that wasn't too bad. The introductions had been made and I was feeling pretty good about it. Although, Frank hadn't given me my kiss goodnight. I had missed that. I didn't know if I could go two months while Jessie was here, without my hugs and kisses. I would have to wait and see how things worked out.

CHAPTER SEVENTEEN

I got up early enough to make sure I saw Frank before he left. "I'm really impressed Angela, Jessie is a credit to you," he said, "I would imagine he will make a wonderful doctor, he seems totally dedicated. He's so young. I knew he would be but he looks even younger than I imagined." "I know what you mean," I said, "he said the same about you." He just smiled, hugged me, kissed me and left for work. Now that was a good way to start the day. Jessie didn't get up until noon and as he came into the kitchen he was still half asleep. "Do you want coffee or tea Jessie?" I said. "Don't worry Mum, I'll make the coffee. I got so used to drinking coffee just to stay awake for exams that I think I have become addicted to it. Beside aren't you going into work today?" He said. "Well, I took the morning off but yes," I said, "I promised I would be in by 1 o'clock to sign some papers. Are you fine on your own? I've filled the fridge with stuff so help yourself. I should be home before 5."

"I might spend some time over at Barry's later on so I'm not too sure if I will be home for dinner, can I let you know later?" He said. "No problem Jessie. You just do whatever you want. You can always have left overs if you're late. It's your time to take a break. It's been a long time since you have been able to spend time with your friends. Well, I'm off to work, take it easy." He gave me a hug and kiss good-by and I was off to work.

How lucky I was. A man that I was in love with and a son that I loved so dearly. I thought about what I had just thought. I actually had said to myself that I was in love with Frank. Oh no, I was going to have to re-think that. I knew that our relationship was different but I couldn't let my emotions get out of control. Good luck on that, I thought. It had taken me 14 years after John died to allow myself be vulnerable. I didn't want to spend another 14 years if Frank left.

CHAPTER EIGHTEEN

The office had started to get busy again but no more than we could handle. When 4:30 came around I was getting ready to leave. I usually left with Mary but when I went into her office she still had papers all over her desk. "What's up Mary, it's time to leave." I said. "Well, Fred's car is in the shop so he has mine. Unfortunately, he got delayed at the factory. He said he wouldn't be here till around 6 o'clock so I thought I would get a start on tomorrows' paper work."

Mary lived a fair distance out of town so there was no bus service in her area and it was out of the question that she wait till her husband arrived, he may take hours. "Here," I said, "you take my car. I wanted to go to the mall anyway. You can drop me off and I'll get the bus home. Don't worry. The bus takes me almost to my door from the mall anyway." "Are you sure?" she said, "it's your new car, I couldn't do that." "Of course you can." I said. "It's a company car and your company. Come on Mary, it's time to go home."

I had planned to go to the mall anyway to buy one of those fancy coffee makers that used a bar code for all that fancy coffee. At least that way I couldn't be blamed if it didn't taste good. If Frank or Jessie didn't like it, they could take it out on the bar code. I had also been thinking of getting back into shape so I could look for something in the sports store. I was in really good shape but I had been eating more than usual. Maybe I should

Tea, Love & Suspicion

get back to playing tennis. I used to like tennis although I hadn't played for some time. I was sure my tennis racket would still be in good condition, so I picked up some new balls. When I left the mall I really wasn't sure about the bus service but at least I knew the number of the bus and really didn't have any problems finding the stop. I was surprised to see just how many people were waiting. As we boarded the bus I was people watching, I loved doing that, trying to see if I could figure out what they did for a living. It looked like we had a good cross section of people although there was one man that bothered me. He had been looking at me, or was I just paranoid? Fortunately it was a short bus ride.

When I got off the bus, it was only a couple of blocks to my home and it wasn't dark yet so I wasn't too worried, however, the strange man that had been looking at me got off at my stop and it made me a little nervous. I kept looking behind me but he wasn't too close so I felt quite safe. As I got closer to my driveway I took one more look behind and although he was still walking my way, he still was far enough away to be safe.

I hurried up the driveway. As I got to my front door I realized that Mary had all my keys. Frank's car wasn't there and nobody answered the bell. I just stood there for a moment and then remembered I had hidden a key on the ledge above the door.

I looked back down the driveway as I reached for the key and didn't see anyone. I took the key and opened the door. Jack, my trusty construction worker used this key to let himself in and out while he was working on Jessie's suite. He had obviously put the key back today after working on my en-suite. Jessie was always guilty of forgetting his key so it had come in handy on more than one occasion. I felt much better when I got inside. I looked back one more time and replaced the key.

My hackles had gone up on my neck when that man got off at my stop so I was right to take precautions but I had watched him as he walked right passed my driveway without a backward glance. I decided I wasn't stable enough to take the bus again and if I had to, I would drive Mary home myself.

Jack had started on my bathroom today and said it would only take a couple of days so not to worry. He made sure that the toilet was the first to be installed but my shower was a different story. When Frank came home from work he was surprised to see me. "Where's your car?" he said. "I didn't think you were home." I explained about Mary and that I had taken the bus from the mall. He gave me my hug and kiss as usual and then asked if it would be okay to take Jessie out for dinner. "Of course," I said, "I'm sure he would love to. Although I don't think he's home yet, he didn't answer the door bell when I rang it."

I headed down stairs and could now hear music coming from his room. No wonder he didn't hear the bell. I asked Jessie if he wanted to go out for dinner with Frank and he said he would love to. As I came back up the stairs Frank had gone to his room to change out of his suit. Two minutes later Jessie came running up the stairs all set to go. I think a ride in Frank's car would have been good enough but to get fed as well, that was great. "I'll have a nice quiet evening, at home," I said, "so you two go have fun." I only partially meant that. I knew that Frank had wanted Jessie to feel comfortable with him living in the house with me when he was gone. I guess this was his way of an introduction. Jessie's father had always taken time to have boys' night out so it really wasn't hard for me to accept. I knew Jessie liked the thought of having a big brother so maybe this would help. Big brother, I thought. Oh boy, I'm in trouble now.

CHAPTER NINETEEN

As they left I planned my evening. I wasn't really hungry as I had had something to eat at the mall so I just had a bowl of soup, toast and tea. When I walked into my en-suite, it was a mess. I thought I should have one of my spa nights so I got my towels, PJ's and dug out the candles and headed to the main bathroom. As I ran the bathtub I placed the candles around the tub and put my bubble bath in.

Just before I got into the tub, my cell phone rang, it was Mary. "Thank you so much Angela, Fred still isn't home yet so I would have still been waiting if you hadn't loaned me your car." "No problem." I said, "I'm just going to have a nice bath and read a book. Frank took Jessie out for dinner so I have the house to myself. I'm going to have myself a spa night." "You do that," said Mary, "I will drop the car off to you tomorrow morning if that's okay?" "Sure," I said, "Saturday is my day to do laundry so I won't be going anywhere." With that we hung up.

Damn, now I needed to go to the Lou before I got into the tub. I wrapped my towel around me and went next door to the Lou. As I sat there contemplating life, I heard a noise. I thought it was Frank and Jessie but they had only been gone for an hour or so. I slowly opened the Lou door to peek out.

To my horror I saw the man from the bus not more than 10 feet from my door. I slammed the door shut and locked it. "Get out here bitch!" He screamed. "Now, get out here or I'll come in and get you." For a moment I froze. Then I realized I still had my cell phone clutched in my hand. I dialled 911. The maniac was pounding on the door and screaming all kinds of obscenities and then I saw a knife blade come through the door panel. I screamed! The 911 operator was calm and I was freaking out. The man's pounding became louder and louder. I wasn't sure how much more the door could take before it broke. "I'm at 562 West Road. Someone broke into my house and wants to kill me." I screamed to the operator. I braced my arms against the narrow wall and put my foot against the door to stop him breaking it down. I was terrified. "The police are on their way Mrs. Bremner, please stay on the line, they should be there in 2 minutes." The 911 operator said. How long is 2 minutes? Not long if you're not facing death but this was the longest 2 minutes in history.

I don't know how long it was but he had almost broken through the panel with his knife and I wondered what I was going to do if the police didn't show up soon. I just kept my arms spread against the wall and my foot on the door and pressed as hard as I could. Then the pounding stopped and I heard screaming and shouting. I heard two gun shots and then quiet.

I looked at my arm and blood was pouring out. It had to be my brachial artery, I had been shot! All of a sudden I came to my senses and realized that I had to stop the bleeding and fast. The blood was running down my body. I unlocked the door, stuck my fist into my arm pit and ran out onto the landing, stark naked. I really didn't realize it at the time but the towel I had on had fallen off long ago.

I quickly rushed over to the table on the landing and grabbed one of the tennis balls I had bought at the mall and stuck it under my arm and clamped it down with my free hand. It was only then that I realized that I had almost tripped over the body of the crazy man and that I was covered in my own blood. Not only that I had three police men looking at me in disbelief. One still had his gun in his hand. I came down into the living room and just at that moment the ambulance arrived and two paramedics came running through the open door.

It was then that I started to feel a little weak. Right behind them was Jessie and Frank. I was really very modest normally, but I now had 7 men in my house and I was stark naked still holding the tennis ball under my arm. I didn't care about the police or the paramedics but Frank and Jessie?

The medics were pretty quick to get to me before I fell but apparently I wouldn't let them take my tennis ball away from me and clamped even harder on the ball. Jessie and Frank were told to get out of the way but they weren't about to leave. I think it was then that I started to feel things going dark. I remember the medics putting me on the gurney and covering me up. Frank stroked my hair and told me I would be okay and Jessie kissed me on the forehead, the only place without blood I think. Jessie said that they would follow us to the hospital and assured me that I would be just fine. He already had that bed side manner I though.

I don't remember anything else after that until I woke up in the hospital. Jessie and Frank were by my side, one on the left and one on the right and they both looked very serious. "I'm alive!" I said as I opened my eyes.

"You were so lucky Mum," Jessie said, "if you hadn't stuck that tennis ball under your arm you may not have made it. The surgeon was really impressed with your quick thinking and said you would be sore but you shouldn't have any complications." "Who shot me?" I said. "It really was an accident." Jessie said. "The officer shot the intruder but one of the bullets went through him and through the door and nicked your brachial." "I was starting to feel really bad for the officer." Frank said.

"He had never had to fire his weapon before and to actually kill someone was bad enough but then he saw you and realized what had happened. Apparently you came running out shouting. "Who the hell shot me?" "I must admit, I really don't remember that part." I said. Obviously I was still recovering from the anaesthetic.

CHAPTER TWENTY

Frank had to leave. It was after 8:00am and he had been here all night. He had to be at a meeting at noon but he had to go home and change. He kissed me on the cheek, I guess he was thinking of Jessie but even in my weakened state I missed that warm reassuring kiss on the lips. He looked into my eyes and I knew he wanted to hold me but he thought better of it, for now.

Just then Mary came running into the room. "Oh my God Angela," she screamed. "I saw the police tape on your front door and Frank's car wasn't there. I almost had a heart attack. The police were still there and they told me that you had been taken to the hospital, so here I am. The police wouldn't tell me a thing." Just then her husband Fred came in. "Well Mum, looks like you have company so maybe I will go home with Frank to take a shower and change and then I will come right back, okay?" "Sure Jessie," I said, "you can take my car. Did you bring my car?" I asked Mary. "Yes, it's outside in the emergency lot." she said. "I even beat Fred here, that car of yours is fast." "No." I said. "It was your lead foot on the pedal." With that Frank and Jessie left.

Mary couldn't contain herself any longer, she was in tears. "Please Angela, please, tell me what happened. I felt sick when I saw police tape around your house, especially when they wouldn't tell me anything." "I'm going to be fine Mary'" I said, "really." "However, it was quite a night. I thought I was going to have a nice relaxing evening but it certainly didn't work out that way. I don't know who the man was but he got into the house and tried to break through my Lou door with a knife. Until the police arrived I thought I was a goner. Actually, you saved me Mary. If I hadn't been on my cell at the time I wouldn't be here now." I was hoping that telling her that may make her feel better. I told her about the man on the bus and how I should have paid more attention to my gut feeling and would pay more attention in the future. We chatted for a while and then I noticed the police officer standing in the doorway. "Hello Mrs. Bremner, remember me?" "Oh yes," I said, "now I remember. How could I ever forget you?" "How are you feeling?" He said. "Are you up to making a statement or would you like me to come back later?" "No, I'm fine," I said, "how long will it take." "Well, that depends on how much you remember." he said. "I'll come back later after your visitors leave."

"Well Angela, Fred and I better get going anyway. Is there anything I can bring for you? Magazines a book or anything you want. I feel like it was my fault that all of this happened." "Don't be crazy Mary, it certainly wasn't your fault, it was that maniac." Mary hugged me and said she would be by tomorrow and to phone her if I needed anything. "That reminds me." I said. "Could you give Jessie a call and ask him to bring in my cell phone, it has all my numbers in it." Mary was still obviously upset. "Okay Angela, I'll phone him on the way home."

The officer stood quietly in the corner of the room until Mary and Fred left. "Let me introduce myself." The officer said. "Mrs. Bremner, my name is Constable Reid." He was so sweet and kept apologizing for having shot me. "If you feel up to it I need to get some details from you about the attack, as much as you can remember, just take your time." "By the way." I said. "My name is Angela." "My name is Robert." He told me that he had just been transferred here a month ago and I could tell that he was still suffering from having shot someone. I went over as much as I could remember from the bus stop to the part when they came through the door. Things were starting to come back to me.

Once we had finished he said that he was sure that there would be somebody coming in to see me, a psychiatrist possibly. He told me he would have to go through a session himself and that he was looking forward to getting it off his chest. "People think we shoot people all the time but most of us never even draw our guns, although I'm glad I did this time." He said. He told me all that he knew about the man who attacked me. Apparently he had been wanted for three other murders in neighbouring towns. He had broken into three other houses where women were alone, raped them, killed them, and robbed them. Up to now nobody had a lead on him so the police force was grateful that I not only survived but had stood my ground and phoned 911. Otherwise, it would have been a totally different story. "Well, thank you Mrs Angela you have been great." Officer Robert said. "If I have any other questions I'll contact you, would that be okay?" "Any time." I said.

Just as he was about to leave, the paramedics came in, the ones from last night. "Just checking on you Mrs Bremner . "How are you? You're looking good." "I'm glad you came by," I said, "I wanted to thank you. You got to me so quickly." It made me realize that without their dedication so many people would have a different ending to their story. We talked for a while and they said how feisty I was and thought the tennis ball should be bronzed or something. I must admit, I thought it was a good idea. They said they would pop in again to see how I was and then they left. I must have slept for a couple of hours, I really was exhausted. I was woken up with a kiss. It was Jessie.

"Well Mum, I checked with the Doctor and he went over everything with me. He told me I should apply to this hospital once I finished college, maybe I could serve my internship here. I told him I still had a long way to go but I was thinking of some nice warm South Pacific island. Actually Mum, I was thinking. I might change my mind about being a surgeon and get into research. Not that your accident changed my mind, I have always wanted to find out why things happen or go wrong in spite of all we know now. Oh well, I have lots of time to make my mind up." "Well Jessie, I want you to remember something. Do what you love to do and you'll do it well and never regret it." I said.

"Oh, by the way Mum, Frank and I were talking and he suggested he take the night shift and I could take the day shift. It's really tiring to have too many visitors at one time and I know Frank would like to spend some time with you. I know you'll have all kinds of company tomorrow, the guys in the office have been calling." That was a strange thing to say. He thought that Frank would like to spend more time with me, but it worked for me. The two most important men in my life looking after me.

Jessie left around 6 o'clock just as Frank was coming in. "See you later Frank." Jessie said as he left. Frank walked a little way down the corridor with Jessie and then came back into the room. He just looked at me for a moment. "Boy Angela, did you scare the hell out of me." He leaned over, held my face in his hands and kissed me. "That was all I needed," I said, "now I feel much better." It suddenly dawned on me that Jessie had been talking to my co-workers in the office. I wondered if they had told him about Frank. Holding hands, going to the movies, dinner, I wondered just how much they had told him, and how much they assumed. When I mentioned my thoughts to Frank he said that Jessie had never mentioned anything but he probably hadn't talked to anyone other than his friends till now.

"Do you know when you'll be getting out?" Frank asked. "Probably Wednesday." I said. I guess I have really good insurance and I really appreciate the private room." Frank held my hand. "I'd like to pick you up when you're ready but I know Jessie wouldn't hear of it. I guess the doctor should be letting you know pretty soon and we can take it from there. Jessie and I are having the house fixed before you come home." He said. "They removed the tape tonight so I guess they have all their information. You may have got yourself injured but really, you probably saved a few lives." "What was the name of my attacker anyway?" "I forgot to ask Robert." Frank looked at me with a, who the heck is Robert look. "Robert is the office who shot me. He came to visit and to get his bullet back." I said. "Funny girl aren't you?" He said as he kissed me. Frank started to tell me all he knew about the maniac. "Well, his name is, was, Thomas Jefferson, believe it or not. Nobody ever believed him apparently but that was really his name. He was well known by the police but until that night, nobody knew where he was till you found him. I have a feeling that you will always be in the good graces of the police." He said.

My time in the hospital went really quickly. I had so many visitors, everybody from the office, Gail and Bert, Mary. Jessie and Frank were a constant. I couldn't wait to get home so I could get some sleep. Dr. Appleby said that I could go home on Wednesday and that I was really healing incredibly well, in fact, he thought I should be as good as new in a week or so, so long as I didn't over-do it. "I could go to work, couldn't I?" I asked. Dr. Appleby looked at me. "Well, maybe for a couple of hours a day would be fine for the first week."

CHAPTER TWENTY ONE

When I got home it was just as if nothing had happened. Except the Lou door had been replaced and new carpet throughout. I don't know how they did it. I think they must have had quite a team working around the clock to get everything done. The carpet, almost the same colour as it was before, had been replaced with new. I really liked the carpet. It was nice to have had it replaced. The Lou door looked different though. Apparently they had to have it made as it wasn't your conventional door. It looked a little more sturdy. Jack had done a good job. When I looked inside I saw that it was much stronger. The original door was 20 years old and it hadn't really been built for battering. The new door should stand up to anything.

"Well Mum, Frank and I are going to take care of you so just sit back and relax. What would you like for lunch?" He said. "Well, I think I would like. A nice cup of tea to start with and then I would like a salad followed by scrambled eggs, sausage, fried tomatoes and finish with rice pudding." "So far Mum, you've got eggs and cheese, how would you really like them?" Poor Jessie he wasn't much of a cook and grilled cheese sandwiches were his speciality. So, I settled for a grilled cheese and tea.

Jessie opened the fridge. "Well Mum, I think I'm just going to go to the store to pick up something special for dinner, what do you think you would like?" he said. Just then the phone rang, Jessie picked it up. "That sounds fantastic." Jessie said as he hung up. "Who was that Jessie?" "That was Frank. He said he is going to pick up something nice for dinner on the way home, I've been saved." I had a bit of a sleep on the sofa and as Frank came through the door he had a whole bunch of bags in his hand. "I know where you've been." I said. He had picked up dinner at the hotel restaurant. Happiness is, I thought, I was starving.

After dinner Jessie asked if he could borrow my car for a couple of hours. He wanted to see Barry and pick up a few DVD's that he had. "Of course Jessie, you do whatever, I'm fine, besides I think Frank will be home anyway." "Sure Mum," he said as he gave me a look. "I won't be too long."

Frank had just come out of the shower and changed into his sweat pants. He had such a beautiful body I thought, long legs, nice, not too hairy chest and that face. Yes, I was getting better. As soon as Jessie left Frank came over and sat beside me on the sofa and put his arm around me. "I thought I knew how much you meant to me," he said, "but when we came home that night and I thought I had lost you I wasn't sure what I was going to do." As he kissed me I could feel things happening in my body that I hadn't felt for 14 years. I started to shake. "Are you okay Angela?" He backed away to look at me. "Yes." I said. "I guess it's probably the anaesthetic wearing off." "Are you sure Angela?" he said. "Yes, I'm fine. It was weird; a shudder just seemed to pass right through me." I was glad that he didn't realize, it had nothing to do with anybody else but him.

Jessie came home at 10 o'clock just after Frank and I had finished watching a great program on TV and we were laughing. "Must be a good one." Jessie said. "It was," I said, "I could watch it all again." I was lucky, most of the programs I liked, so did Frank. "How was your visit with Barry?" I asked Jessie. "How was the baby this time?" "Well, the baby is almost sleeping through the night and we didn't hear a peep out of him. They look so cute when they're sleeping but I was glad he didn't wake up. I guess Barry and Patricia managed to work through their problems and now Barry has at least one night looking after James and so does she. The rest of the time they share all of the responsibilities. It seems to be working out thank goodness. I really can't take it when people argue." "Me neither." I said.

We sat talking for a while and then I started to feel really tired. I think I over did it a little. "Come on Mum, I'll help you up to your room." "Goodnight Frank." I said. "See you tomorrow." He looked at me and then he looked at Jessie. "Yes." he said as he diverted his eyes. Jessie guided me up the stairs to my room. I was sure I would be more like myself tomorrow. As I walked into my en suite I marvelled at how beautiful it looked now. Jack had outdone himself. In fact, he had done more than I had asked for. As I climbed into bed I think I was asleep before my head hit the pillow.

CHAPTER TWENTY TWO

I woke up early feeling great although I had been woken up a few times as I turned over onto my bad arm. I could hear someone in the kitchen, it had to be Frank. I splashed some water on my face, combed my hair and brushed my teeth and walked into the kitchen. "I love this coffee maker you got," Frank said, "every cup tastes just as good as the last one." "You know." I said. "If I didn't make such rotten coffee I wouldn't have been so eager to buy that coffee maker then I wouldn't have bought the tennis balls. So there, it was meant to be." "I just love your logic Angela."

Frank came over and looked at me. I didn't move. It seemed like a long time before he put his arms gently around me and gave me a huge kiss that seemed to last forever. "I have to go out of town the day after tomorrow." He said. "I'll only be gone a couple of days but will you be okay?" "Sure I will," I said, "I feel great and Jessie will be around and besides, I was planning to start going into the office tomorrow."

Mary had planned to pick me up and drop me off until I could get this arm moving properly. I felt so good but I didn't want to rip the stitches out. It's a good thing I still have a good right arm I thought, I'm really useless with my left. "I'll mention to Jessie that you'll be away for a few days." I said. "He seems to like the idea of having someone else around to help out even though I've been on my own for so long and managed pretty well." "You really are an independent woman Angela." Frank said. "It's part of your charm." He said as he kissed me on the forehead.

"Gadda go to work." he said. "Call me later and if you don't call me, I'll call you." "Okay." I said as I walked him to the door to get my kiss. I really liked kissing. I thought to myself. It was a new thing for me after so many years. Nobody would have believed me but I hadn't kissed one person other than Jessie in 14 years, nor had I made love to anyone. Who would ever believe me? I think I was scared to even think about it. In fact, I was beginning to think that kissing was even better than making love. And, I wasn't planning on taking my relationship with Frank any further. For now.

I still felt like there was something I didn't know about him. I should have followed my intuition when I saw that Thomas Jefferson. I felt it, but although I didn't ignore it, I should have done something different. It wasn't the same feeling I had about Frank, it was just a tingle I felt on my neck. I had nothing to base it on but isn't that what intuition is I thought.

Jessie didn't get up until just before I was about to leave for work. Mary had already phoned me and would be here in about 15 minutes. "Where are you going Mum?" Jessie said. "I'm just going into the office for a couple of hours. Mary is picking me up and dropping me off later." "I'll pick you up." Jessie said. Mary doesn't have to bother and I have your car anyway. Just phone me when you're ready to leave." "Sounds good to me," I said, "I'll call you later." "Oh, by the way, Frank is leaving on business tomorrow for a couple of days he told me to let you know so you can take care of me. How'd you like that?" "I always wanted a bossy big brother Mum, now maybe I have one."

CHAPTER TWENTY THREE

As I walked into the office everyone gathered around me. Some of them that visited me in the hospital had already been given the story but now they wanted to know who the man was that attacked me. "His name is Thomas Jefferson believe it or not and he was a real low life." I said. "He had brutally killed three other women that they even knew of for sure. But at least he won't hurt anyone else." "Did you see the dead body Angela?" Francis said. "Well, kind of." I said. "I almost tripped over him. Apparently I was screaming obscenities at him when I came out of the Lou." It's funny, I thought, how I had what they call selective memory. I remember some things quite clearly and other things are just a blur. "I hear you were naked." Frances said. "Well, yes, I was but I didn't really notice it at first until I saw the three policemen and the paramedics and, well, enough about that." I said. "I'm sure you read the paper." "Just about the whole paper was about you and how brave you were," said Mary. "Not brave," I said, "scared stiff is more like it. Well it's all over now and I'm feeling pretty good." I said as I walked back into my office.

Everyone went back to what they were doing and I spent the next couple of hours sorting out some papers and signing checks. I decided to phone Jessie and have him pick me up. I had done enough for today. It only took Jessie about 15 minutes to show up in the office. "Hello everybody." He said.

It looked like everybody stood up together to visit with Jessie. He was such a sociable kid. "Well, we better get going Mum, I'm almost double parked." "Somehow I think your mother has some friends in the police department now," said Mary, "not to worry." "Hum," Jessie said. "No," I said, "don't even think about it." I was one of those people who lived by the rules and couldn't understand why other people liked to break them.

As we drove away from the office Jessie said that he had already stopped off at the store and picked up something for dinner. As we pulled into the driveway Franks' car was already there. He's early I thought, he's usually not home until 6 o'clock. As we walked in the door Frank was on his cell phone, or lifeline as I called it. He saw us come in and went straight into his bedroom and closed the door. I don't know why he was in such a rush. That was the first time he had done that and I could feel that tingling on the back of my neck again. Don't be silly I said to myself. Although it was no wonder I was sensitive after what I had just been through. Everything just seemed to be magnified.

He was only in his room for a few minutes and came out to see me. "How was your day?" he said. He gave me a little hug and walked into the kitchen and put the kettle on. "I only worked for a couple of hours today and I think that was enough for one day. I'll probably spend more time tomorrow. How was your day, your home early?" I said. "Pretty good I guess. I have a few things to sort out but nothing I can't handle." He said. It was strange, I noticed a little hesitation in his voice but his business was his business and I let it go. "Teas on." said Frank in a much more cheerful tone. I think he saw the look on my face and decided to lighten the conversation a little.

"You were all the talk around the plant today Angela, even the old timers were talking about it." Frank said. "It's funny, I have never seen such a small newspaper, ever, and it would seem that everybody in town has a copy and actually reads it." "Boring" said Jessie. "Not you Mum; I mean the newspaper in general. I guess nothing really happens here. This must be the most interesting piece of news since 1920 when a guy went on a shooting spree with his shotgun."

We all sat around the kitchen table and Jessie was mentioning some of the things he bought in the store. "It's not really dinner time yet but I'm getting hungry." Jessie said. "I might as well start getting something ready." As Frank walked out of the kitchen he looked back at Jessie. "Give me a few minutes Jessie, I'll just have a quick shower and change and we can both work on it." "You, Miss Angela go sit and watch the TV or something. We'll put something together, you just relax." How could I not, I could actually get used to this although I didn't know what the main course was going to be yet. I did know, however, that whatever it was I would have to eat it, even if I didn't like it.

It really didn't turn out too bad. The salad was good but the macaroni and cheese was never one of my favourites. "I cook this all the time at school." Jessie said. "I really got to like it. I got pretty good at BBQ too so maybe I can pick up some steaks tomorrow and roast some potatoes." "I'll be gone early tomorrow so count me out." said Frank. "I have to leave around 6am." Jessie was busy setting the table. "That is early Mum, what time are you going to work?" "I planned to go in around 9 o'clock. If you want, you can drive me to work and you can have the car for the day or at least until 3:00."

The dishes got put in the dishwasher and we all sat down to watch TV. It wasn't a good night for TV, they were all re-runs, what else is new, I thought. It seems they have more re-runs than they have new stuff. It was only 9 o'clock and Frank said he was going to bed. He said his goodnights and went to his bedroom. Jessie looked at me. "Does Frank seem a little down tonight Mum, he's usually pretty talkative?" "Maybe it's something at work." I said. "I've had days like that myself but nobody was around to see, so I just had to grin and bear it." "What does he do anyway?" Jessie asked. "Well, I don't really know. I thought it must be something to do with his car but I've never even asked him. I suppose if I asked him he would tell me but I keep thinking it might be some secret development and he just can't talk about it so I don't ask." "Hum," said Jessie, "maybe your right, that car certainly is pretty special."

"Well, I think I will go listen to some music in my room mum, do you need anything before I go?" "No thanks Jessie, I can manage. Don't forget I want to be in the office at 9 o'clock so if you want the car you better get up early and drive me?" "Okay Mum, it's a deal, I'll set my alarm."

Two minutes after Jessie left, Frank came out of his room. "You still up Angela, I thought you would be in your own bed by now, can I get you anything?" "No thanks," I said, "I might make another cup of tea in a minute or so but that's all. I think I'll have an early night too." Frank walked into the kitchen and put the kettle on and I followed right behind him. "Are you all right Frank, you seem a little out of sorts tonight." "I'm fine." He said, "I'm just in the middle of negotiating a big contract and I want to make sure that I have all my ducks in a row before I get to this meeting."

With that he came over to me and held me. I think that it was as much for him as it was for me. He kissed me softly and then he kissed me again only this time I could feel his hold on me tightening as if he were trying to let me know how much he felt, but didn't say. "I wanted to do that hours ago," he said, "but I thought Jessie might get the wrong message." "I'm not too sure what message Jessie is getting." I said. "We haven't talked about us living in the same house. He just seems to accept it so I haven't brought up the subject either." "What will you tell him if he asks?" Frank said. "I really don't know. There really

Tea, Love & Suspicion   **69**

isn't anything to say." I said. "I guess you're right." Frank said.
"Well, I'll be back some time Friday night so you and Jessie can
have some alone time, I think he likes looking after you for a
change." With that, he went to his room and I went to mine.

CHAPTER TWENTY FOUR

I slept like a baby, no dreams, no nightmares and felt better than I had for days. I glanced over at the clock and it was only 5 o'clock. I listened to see if I could hear Frank in the kitchen but the house was quiet. I went to the bathroom and looked into the mirror. Sleepy face never did look good so I washed my face and put some face cream on trying to smooth things out. My hair looked like a rats nest, I must have had one heck of a night, I had to use my brush to get it untangled. By the time I brushed my teeth I was feeling pretty good. I kept thinking that in order for me to sleep like a baby I would wake up looking like an old lady. Maybe too much sleep was over-rated.

As I was walking into the kitchen Frank came out of his room. "What are you doing up so early?" he said. "I just felt so good when I woke up I wanted to enjoy it." I said. I don't think I slept at all," Frank said. "That's unusual for me, I could normally sleep through a hurricane but I guess every once in a while it makes you feel grateful for the good sleep you do get. He walked over to the coffee maker. "I'm just going to have a quick cup of coffee to wake me up before I go, join me with your tea before I leave?" His phone dinged. It was someone from his office letting him know that the car would be there to pick him up in 2 minutes. He drank his coffee so fast I hadn't hardly started my tea when he got up to leave. "Do you have everything?" I said. "Yup, it's all in here." He patted his

Tea, Love & Suspicion   71

suitcase." I followed him to the door, waiting for my kiss, but it didn't happen. I was just about to close the door when he came running back in. "You don't think I forgot do you?" With that he gave me the kiss I was expecting. "See you Friday." He said, as he made his way to his ride, then he was gone.

I wasn't too sure what time Frank was coming back so I wasn't too concerned when he wasn't home by 10 pm. By midnight I was beginning to wonder, did something happen to him, did he miss his flight and why did he not call to let me know. I decided to check his room, it was locked. I noticed that the door lock had been changed and I was a little surprised. I thought maybe he had it changed after we had the episode with Thomas Jefferson but I wish he had told me. It was almost 2am before I eventually decided to go to bed. I lay there thinking that even if he was hurt or dead I wouldn't begin to know who to contact. I eventually drifted off to sleep. When I woke up I thought of trying his door again but what would I do if he was in there so I decided to wait and see. He had got a ride to the airport so it was no use looking to see if his car was there, it was.

It was the longest day I think I have ever spent. I did my usual that I had done with Jessie. First I got worried. Then I got angry for being so inconsiderate. Did he not think I was worried? Was he coming back? Ever since I had got to know him I had a thought in the back of my mind that he would eventually leave, maybe I was right. Maybe this was it.

After I had breakfast I decided to try his cell phone. It went to "this customer is not available at this time." I hated that, why do people shut their phone off, especially Frank, it was his lifeline. By noon Jessie eventually came up for breakfast. "Hi Mum what's up?" "Frank didn't come back last night," I said, "and he hasn't phoned. I hope he's okay." I didn't want Jessie to know just how much I was worried. "He's a big boy Mum, I'm sure he's just fine." It was easy for him to say, but he was right. Frank was a big boy and he was free to come and go and he really didn't have to answer to me.

I jumped when the phone rang and rushed to answer it. "Oh, hello Barry, yes, Jessie's home I'll call him." It seemed like Jessie was on the phone forever. I didn't want to ask him to hang up but I was getting really anxious. At last, he hung up the phone. "Are you going out today Mum?" Jessie said. "No, I don't think so, I have a few things to do around the house and yes, you can take the car." I already knew what he was going to ask so I thought I would save him the trouble. "If you want to lend me your cell phone you can call me if you need your car." Jessie said. "No." I said rather quickly. "You phone me. What time are you leaving?" Jessie walked over to the door. "Pretty soon, in fact now. Do you need anything before I leave mum?" "No," I said, "but phone me before you come home just in case."

As he left I looked at the time. It was 2pm and sill no Frank. By 4 o'clock, I was a mess and I was getting really angry with myself for caring so much. The phone rang and I just about jumped out of my seat. "Hello Jessie." I said. "No, it's not Jessie." The caller said. "Who is this?" I said. "It's Frank; I thought you would recognize my voice by now."

"Sorry I didn't phone earlier, I'll fill you in when I get there." "Where are you?" I said. He told me he was at the airport just waiting for his ride and that he would be home in an hour or so. I could feel my whole body relax but I was still fuming that he had taken so long to let me know he was still alive and obviously well. I couldn't wait until he got home; I thought I might just beat him up. By the time he arrived my anger had subsided. I could never be angry for long anyway but I did want to know why he didn't call me.

As he came through the door he dropped his suitcase, gave a quick look around for Jessie and lifted me off the ground. "It's good to be back." He said as he planted a kiss on me that just

Tea, Love & Suspicion 73

about knocked my socks off. He kissed me three times, picked me up again and took me into the kitchen. "I'm dying for a cup of coffee." He said. "How about you?" He was on such a high I thought a cup of coffee would take him over the edge. "We got the contract." He blurted out. "We should have it ready for signing within the month." I didn't have the heart to get mad at him, I thought that maybe he knew me only too well. He was smart, maybe too smart for me.

"What time would you like to go for dinner?" he said. "I'm starving so anytime is good for me." I wasn't able to eat lunch so I was ready to go. "Give me a couple of minutes to have a shower and change." He said. "Me too." We both left to get ready. "Where are we going?" I shouted to him. "I thought I felt like a nice big steak at the Hotel, is that fine with you?" "Sounds good." I said. I would have to get a little bit more dressed up for the hotel so I chose my simple black dress, my favourite for all occasions. We both hit the shower at the same time. It used to be a problem but I had Jack install an immersion heater in my bathroom. It was nice to be able to use both showers without freezing or getting that cold shower I hated. Jessie always ran the hot water tap on purpose just to hear me scream.

CHAPTER TWENTY FIVE

It was 7 o'clock by the time we left for the Hotel. As we walked into the hotel, there was Tom to greet us. "Good evening Mr. Winston, Ma'am." he said as we walked towards the restaurant. "Good evening Tom." I said. He just nodded. We started with salad and neither of us said a word until we finished. We were obviously hungry. As we waited for our main course Frank told me more in the next 15 minutes about his business than he had in the whole time I had known him.

Apparently he had had a meeting with the U.S. representatives of a German company and they had agreed on a personal meeting to sign a contract. It should be ready within the next couple of weeks. It sounded like it was a done deal but not until they all signed the contract. Still, it sounded like things would start rolling at the plant once the contract was in place. He was still talking through bites of his steak and right through desert. Although he talked a lot, I still didn't know exactly what it was that he would be manufacturing, but I didn't ask. It was the first time he had opened up to me about his business and I thought I would let him spill it out in his own time.

On the way home Frank took a different route and seemed to be looking in his rear view mirror. He actually pulled over at one point and got out of the car. He walked around and was looking under the car. I couldn't imagine what could be wrong, I hadn't noticed any strange noise or anything but Frank had all those dials he kept checking. "What's wrong?" I said. "Nothing, I just thought I felt something." He said. He stopped talking as a car passed us and watched it disappear in the distance. I could feel that he was concerned about something but as soon as he got into the car his attitude was back to happy. Either he's a really good actor or I'm imagining things I thought.

As we got closer to the house Frank asked me if it was possible to put his car in the garage. I really hadn't used it for a while so I said yes. Another weird thing, why would he want to hide his car? "I hope you don't mind." he said. "The sap from the trees has been driving me crazy and if I don't keep washing it, it might cause a problem with the paint." I really thought that his paint job was made of Teflon, it looked thick and shiny and it always looked clean but maybe he had it washed every day at the plant. That wasn't unreasonable. "I'll get you the clicker for the door." I said as he waited for me to come back.

The clicker didn't work. "Must be the batteries." I said. "I'll be back in a minute." Sure enough, it was the batteries. I went in behind the car and we went through the inside door to the house. John had always parked in the garage but I usually parked in the car port unless the weather was bad. We had a larger than normal two car garage. Not like those iddy biddy ones we saw in England, so there was lots of room if I wanted to use it. I think when John had it built he was thinking trucks rather than cars.

When Jessie came home he was surprised to see Frank sitting at the kitchen table. "When did you get in?" he said. "We were getting worried, did something happen to your car?" Frank got up to pour himself another coffee. I didn't get back till around 6 o'clock. I was delayed with meetings and couldn't get away so I missed my flight. And as for my car, it's in great shape Frank said. Also, while I'm on the subject. So long as nobody minds I'm going to be parking my car in the garage for now.

Too much sap from the trees. By the way Jessie, did you park in the driveway or in front of the garage? I'll probably be leaving early so I don't want to wake you up." "No problem." Jessie said. "I'll move it right now." I thought that Jessie responded more quickly to Frank than he did me. He would have probably said "In a minute mum." and I would usually have to ask him again.

When Jessie came back in I asked him if he was hungry. "No, actually Patricia made dinner for us tonight." he said. It was great, except for the Brussels sprouts. Barry found a great wife. She's really pretty, when she's not angry, she's funny and it turns out she's a good cook. Just like you mum and by the way. I was thinking of visiting with Grandma and Grandpa before I go back to school." Jessie planned to stay with them for a week or so because he probably wouldn't be able to see them for quite some time once his studies began again. "I'm really looking forward to seeing them so I thought that I would leave in a couple of weeks. If that's fine with you? "Of course it is." I said. He came over and gave me a hug. "I would imagine they still have that lumpy single bed so I am going to miss my room." "By the way mum, if I haven't thanked you enough, I love it downstairs, in fact, I am going there right now so I can savour the splendour while I can." He kissed me on the forehead and went to his room.

It was already late and I could tell that Frank was starting to fade fast. "I think it's time for me to say goodnight too Frank." I was exhausted. Its funny how when you're really happy or really anxious once you relax, the body just starts to eventually shut down. Frank stood up just before I did and came over to me. "I'm sorry if you were worried about me when I didn't come back on Friday but things were crazy and I had left my charger in my hotel room. Forgive me?" I stood up and wrapped my arms around him. He put his hand under my chin and lifted my face. As I looked into those beautiful eyes, I melted. I felt like a

Tea, Love & Suspicion

little girl when he towered over me. He had to bend over to kiss me and again, I felt that old feeling return.

CHAPTER TWENTY SIX

The next couple of weeks went quickly. Jessie was off to visit his grandparents and Frank and I had been working like crazy. He was expecting the representative flying in from Germany in a couple of days so some nights he didn't get home until 7 o'clock. I was surrounded by papers when Frank phoned me at work. "How about we go to the Hotel tonight for dinner? It's been a while and I don't know about you but I need a break." "Me too." I said. "Just let me know once you're on your way."

As we walked into the hotel, as usual Tom was there to greet us. "Good evening Mr. Winston." We always sat at the same table. It had become a ritual so we just walked into the restaurant and sat down. No sooner had we sat down when Frank noticed someone looking at us. The man walked slowly over to our table. "Mr. Winston?" he said. "Yes, can I help you?" Frank said. "I'm Dr. Winterhoff," he said. "I hope you don't mind this interruption but I came in a couple of days early to visit your beautiful town and relax before our meeting on Monday. My secretary and I were going to contact you tomorrow but when I heard your name I thought it would be impolite of me not to introduce myself."

It turned out he was the man Frank was supposed to meet to sign the contract but that was supposed to be Monday and this was only Friday. Maybe that was a good thing. Signed sealed and delivered a couple of days early. "Have you eaten?" Frank asked. "Yes." said Winterhoff. "We ate earlier. Maybe we can join you for coffee later if you wish." "That would be perfect." said Frank. With that Winterhoff went back to his table to join his secretary. "He speaks almost perfect English Frank. You could hardly hear the accent." I said. "It's a good thing," said Frank, "because I don't speak one word of German. I've spoken to him on the phone on a number of occasions but he's quite articulate in person." Just then our meal arrived.

Once we had finished Frank went over to Winterhoff's table and ask them to join us. "Good evening again." he said to me. "My name is Horst Winterhoff and let me introduce my secretary Frau Weisinger." Frau Weisinger didn't speak much English but I am sure she understood a lot of our conversation. Winterhoff was very sociable.

"We were planning to take a sight-seeing boat tomorrow." he said. "I have heard it is quite beautiful and we may even see some whales, is this true?" Frank looked at me for the answer. He knew I had been a boater with John and I knew my way around the marina. "Yes," I said, it's quite possible. I heard there was a sighting just yesterday. Have you made arrangements to rent your vessel yet?" "No, actually I was going to ask the front desk if they could help with that, they seem very helpful." "Well, I do know of a good rental company and they supply lunches and even dinners if you wish." I said. "I could give them a call in the morning to see if they are available." "That would be very kind of you but why don't we all go? We could take the contract with us and relax on the boat." he said. "That would be perfect." Frank said. Frank looked at me. "I'll phone them in the morning." I said. "Frank will let you know if it's available and what time. Would that be acceptable?" "That would be perfect." Winterhoff said. "And now, I hope you will excuse us, it has been a very long day for us."

They bowed and left. I could almost hear Winterhoff's heels click. I looked at Frank. "I gather you weren't expecting them to arrive so soon." I said. Frank was signing for our meal. "No," he said, "I wasn't, but the sooner we sign the contract the sooner we can get started."

CHAPTER TWENTY SEVEN

When we got home Frank was in a good mood. "Let me know if you can arrange for a boat for tomorrow afternoon, maybe after lunch would be good and possibly have dinner on board." He said. "I'll charge it all to the company so the sky's the limit." He looked at me for an answer. "I'll call first thing. It isn't really tourist season yet so there should be something good available, I'll let you know." I said. We both plunked ourselves on the sofa and sighed.

"You know what?" Frank said. "Jessie has left the building and we have the whole house to ourselves. I can kiss you, I can attack you I can hold you and what's more…" He started to rough house with me and we ended up on the floor. He was on top of me and he weighed a ton but I didn't move. We kissed and hugged and were almost to the point of no return when I moved and lay by his side. We both realized that we better stop before it went any further so we just held each other and lay quiet for a while. It felt good. How could I have thought he was gay, well, it had been months since we met and most couples would have been having sex on the second date, sometimes the first date. I was beginning to wonder if there was something wrong with me. I didn't think so. I had the yearning but there was always something held in reserve. I still had my doubts about who he was and until I felt secure I would avoid what might seem to be the inevitable as long as I could. We actually fell asleep on the floor, still holding each other. Frank was the first to wake up and he carried me to my bed and left me. I thought I better set my alarm so I could make arrangements for the boat.

I just about jumped out of my skin when the alarm went off. I was in such a deep sleep. It took me a minute to collect my thoughts. Oh yes, I thought I better phone the charter company and see what they had available.

They answered on the first ring. "Hello, this is Mrs. Bremner is Richard still with you?" I asked. "Yes, this is Richard." How are you Mrs. Bremner, it's been a long time since I heard from you." "Your right Richard, it's been much too long. I was wondering if you had a sail boat available to rent for today." "Did you want to sail it yourself Mrs. Bremner or would you need a crew?" "It's been too long Richard, yes, I would really like a crew, do you have anyone in mind?" "I think so. I have the boat but I would have to check on the crew. Did you want to be fed and how many people are in your party?" "There will be four of us," I said, "and, if possible, we would like to have dinner on board." "Let me get back to you and I will see what I can do for you. It really is good to hear from you again and I will do my very best."

I gave him my number and headed for the shower. It felt so good to have a shower and by the time I came into the kitchen Frank was up and making breakfast. "Scrambled eggs, toast and tea." He said. "That sounds fantastic, I'm famished." I said.

I filled him in about booking the sail boat and we started our breakfast. We had just finished when the phone rang. "It's Richard Mrs. Bremner, I have a crew all set and we are just going to get some provisions for the trip. Is there anybody that might be allergic to something that I should watch out for?" "No," I said, "not that I know of with the exception of peppers of any colour." I turned to Frank. "Are you allergic to anything else?"

Tea, Love & Suspicion

"Nope, just peppers." "That was easy," Richard said. "What time would you like to come aboard?" "Can I call you back on that?" I said. "I would think around 2 o'clock but I'll check back with you in a couple of minutes."

Frank phoned Winterhoff at the hotel and he thought that would be perfect, we could pick them up after lunch around 1:30.

Dinner on board around 5:00 would be great. It was all set. I was really looking forward to sailing again, we used to have our own boat and John and I loved it. We had taken all the courses and we turned out to be pretty good sailors, but that was a long time ago.

CHAPTER TWENTY EIGHT

Frank and I picked up Winterhoff and Weisinger at the hotel. Frank always drove my car when we were together. He said my car was a dream to drive he didn't have to keep checking those indicators. He just had to turn it on and point it in the right direction. My car was less than a year old and although I loved driving it myself I was more than willing to let Frank drive. When Winterhoff got into the car he remarked on the leather seats. "Nice car," he said, "I always did like the BMW." As we pulled into the marina it really was a beautiful sight. I'd forgotten how much I loved it. We went over to the office to sign the papers and meet the crew. I noticed that our captain was an old friend. "Hugh," I said, "it's good to see you again, just can't retire can you?" "No." he said. I'm like the old man from sea. I just love it so much." "I can understand." I said as we headed to the dock. Before we knew it we were on our way. The sail boat was beautiful and the day was perfect, it was like sailing on a pond. Too bad we couldn't use the sails but there was no wind. "Hello," this little voice said. "My name is Jenny, I'll be bringing you some finger food shortly and we have red or white wine and other drinks at the bar. Could I get you anything right now?" We opted for some white wine and she brought some cheese and crackers, stuffed mushrooms and a variety of potato chips.

We had a little wine and decided to go top side to see the scenery. It was gorgeous, but we didn't see any whales. We

Tea, Love & Suspicion   **85**

were about an hour out and we headed down to the galley. Winterhoff reached into his brief case and brought out the contract. "Did you get your e-mailed copy of the contract yet?" he asked. "Yes," Frank said. "I went over it yesterday and everything seems to be in order. My lawyer thought it was pretty straight forward." Winterhoff turned to his secretary and said something in German. It was a dialect that I understood because both my mother and father were from that region. He had said to Frau Weisinger that "he had it made and that before long they would be rich."

I shot a look at Frank as he picked up the pen. Winterhoff had already marked all of the x's where he was to sign. Frank was just about to sign when we heard a blood curdling scream.

Frank and I ran up to the wheel house and there was Hugh on the floor. He looked blue. I had updated my CPR a few months ago so without thinking I felt for a pulse, nothing and he wasn't breathing either. I asked Jenny if they had a medical kit on board and she pointed behind me. "Get me that kit." I ordered Frank. "Do either of you know CPR?" I asked. They both shook their heads. Winterhoff and his secretary were still down stairs doing who knows what and I didn't have time to bother with them. I looked into the kit and found a mouth piece and inserted it into Hugh's mouth and started to breath into it.

"Call the coast guard Jenny and tell them what's going on, make it an emergency." I said rather sharply. Fortunately Jenny knew how to contact the Coast Guard and they said they were on their way. "Do you have any oxygen Jenny?" I asked between compressions. "Over there," she said. "Well get it!" I shouted. I may have some apologies after this was over but for now, I was in charge. Poor Hugh, I had worked on him for 30 minutes and I got absolutely no response. I knew I should wait until a doctor or someone in authority said quit but I just couldn't do it anymore and I honestly believed he had been gone before he even hit the floor.

All this time we had been slowly sailing out to sea and I knew I had to come about. I just hoped I remembered what to do. I looked at the controls and as luck would have it, they really hadn't changed since John and I had owned one. I started my turn around. We were so lucky that the sea was so calm because if it was rough I would have had a big problem. We were on our way back to the marina when the coast guard showed up.

One of their crew boarded the boat and took over the controls. We had covered Hugh up with a blanket but left him as he fell. "We have notified the police and ambulance that we are on our way in but unfortunately it's a little late for Hugh." the officer said. "I really liked that old man but I guess he died doing what he loved to do. Lucky for everyone you knew what to do Ma'am, you did a good job of coming to us."

As we came into the dock, I could see the police car and ambulance. The same ones that had been at my house. "Hello Robert. Not good to see you." I said. Frank helped me onto the dock and Winterhoff and Weisinger were right behind us. They had stayed below deck for all this time. I heard Winterhoff say "Let's get out of here and fast." I was just about to tell Frank when Robert, my friendly policeman came up to me and asked exactly what had happened.

Frank and I gave him all the information and he told us that he would need us at the station to fill out an incident report. Poor Jenny, I had almost forgotten about her. She was standing leaning against a post crying. "I am so sorry," I said, "both for your loss and for the way I was shouting at you." I took her into my arms and she sobbed uncontrollably. She hadn't cried until they came past her with the gurney with Hugh's' lifeless body. She was probably the bravest of us all. It was only then that I looked around for Winterhoff. He was nowhere to be seen. "Did

Tea, Love & Suspicion

you see Winterhoff? I said to Frank. "No, I haven't," he said, "where did they go? I thought they were still here?" "Nope," I said, "and somehow I think this may be your lucky day."

CHAPTER TWENTY NINE

We looked all over the marina for Winterhoff and Weisinger but they were nowhere to be found. "Well, maybe they went back to the hotel." Frank said. "Maybe." was all I could say, so we drove to the hotel. We didn't have to give our written statement to the police till the next day so there was no rush.

We arrived at the hotel and parked. As we walked in Tom was standing in the doorway. "Back again Sir, Ma'am." he said. "Yes Tom, have you seen that couple that we left with this afternoon," I said. "Yes, you just missed them; they left for the airport about 20 minutes ago." "What!" Frank exclaimed. "What the hell is going on?" "I think there was something wrong with those two." I said. "I only heard them talk to each other a couple of times but I got the feeling they were up to no good." "Do you speak German?" Frank said. "Yes, I speak it fluently. They actually spoke the same dialect that my parents speak. It's not high German," I said, "it's a local language from where I was born." Frank looked at me. "Angela, you have surprised me so many times today I'm blown away."

He started walking back to the car muttering to himself. "I better phone the head of the company in Germany and find out what is going on. I know Winterhoff's voice sounded different but I thought it was just because of the conference call distortion. The only problem is, it's in the wee small hours of Sunday morning over there and I can't call anybody." "Bloody Hell!" he

Tea, Love & Suspicion

said. At last I thought I had taught Frank something. Bloody Hell was my favourite British expression when things weren't going right and right now it seemed really appropriate.

As we walked to the car I could tell Frank was so frustrated he couldn't stand still. As we got into the car he turned to me and said. "You know what Angela. If it hadn't been for Hugh dying there's a possibility I might have signed that contract. Who knows what the heck might have happened if I had signed."

By the time we got home he was starting to settle down. "Well, let's see what Monday has to bring, they were supposed to arrive Monday afternoon. I was going to pick them up at the airport. He interrupted himself. "By the way," he said. "While I'm on the subject, could I use your car to pick them up?" "Sure," I said. "I'll have Mary pick me up, she owes me one." "Your car does have limitations doesn't it?" I said. Frank looked at me and grabbed my leg. "It fits you and me like a glove doesn't it?" he said, "and that's good enough for me."

CHAPTER THIRTY

As we drove into the driveway Frank was all wound up. "I really need a drink. Do you have anything at the house or should I go back to the hotel to pick something up?" "I don't have much," I said, "just what was left after Margaret's tribute. That should be enough don't you think?" "Maybe, I'll let you know." he said. Neither of us drank, except for the odd glass of wine with dinner and unless Jessie had found the stash I should have something left.

As we walked through the door it was as if someone had turned on a light and I felt my whole body relax. I hadn't realized that I was so tense but I could see the same reaction in Frank. "We need a hug Frank," I said. As he held me I started talking into his chest. "You know what Frank. My life was pretty boring till I met you. You're good for me. I think." We stood in one spot for at least 5 minutes, just holding each other. Eventually Frank let go and said, "Where's the booze?" "I'll get it for you. I put it in the back of the cupboard in the kitchen."

There was a little of this and a little of that but enough to make me sick I thought. "It's all yours." I said until I saw the bottle of St. Reme Brandy. I picked it up and looked at it. There wasn't much and who knows how long it had been sitting there. All of a sudden I felt sad, it reminded me of John. If we had had a difficult day we would come home, light the fire and have a snifter of Brandy. "Thinking of John, aren't you?" Frank said.

Tea, Love & Suspicion 91

"Yes how did you know?" Frank came closer. "Well sometimes when Jessie talks about his father, you get that look on your face, are you alright." "Yes, it was just a moment of thought for a wonderful man." "You're lucky you know Angela, it's very rare that anyone has had such a love in their life." Frank said as he gave my hand a squeeze.

"By the way, how is your arm doing? You seemed to have recovered so fast." "Once in a while I get a twinge," I said, but really, I was lucky to have it repair so quickly. I sometimes forget it happened. I guess Dr. Appleby did a good job and the shrink said I was a well centered individual, how about that!"

I lit the fire and we sat down to watch TV and tried to forget the day. How could so many things happen in one day? Frank interrupted my thoughts. "By the way Angela. After I pick up the guys from Germany." "Guys," I said, don't they have names?" "To tell you the truth I'm not sure anymore." Frank said. "Anyway, as I was saying, after I pick them up I want to take them to the hotel to rest and meet them for dinner. Would you please come with me? You can be my Weisinger." I smacked him on the arm but told him I would. I couldn't wait to hear what they had to say about their impostors.

The television was on but I don't think we heard a word. We were both in our own world. I stretched out on the sofa and put my head in Franks lap. He gently stroked my hair and I fell fast asleep. I must have only slept for a few minutes but all of a sudden I sat up and decided it was time to go to bed. "Good night Frank, I'm off to bed, I'm totally exhausted." "Me too," he said, "I feel like I've been hit by a truck." For all we had been through today it's no wonder we were worn out. "I'll walk you to the door." he said as he helped me up the stairs. "Night Night." I said. "See you in the morning." It was a brief kiss tonight but never the less I needed it, it had become such a habit. I really had a workout trying to revive Hugh so I thought I should have a shower before I went to bed and hoped it wouldn't wake me up. I could wash my hair tomorrow.

CHAPTER THIRTY ONE

I really did have a good sleep but I think I passed out rather than went to sleep. As I climbed out of bed the next morning I could hear that Frank was already in the kitchen. I had a quick shower, washed my hair and decided to let it dry on its own. It was going to be my, let it all hang out day and I climbed into my sweat suit. The kettle was boiling as I walked into the kitchen and Frank was already sitting drinking his coffee. "That coffee smells pretty good, I wish I liked it," I said, "how long have you been up?" "About an hour," he said, "I think I had a good sleep but I don't remember. I was sleeping." "You're funny this morning." I said, "Do you have any plans for the day?" "No, I tried phoning Germany, there was no answer so I left a message for them to call me. I didn't go into any details, just a call to confirm their arrival time. I'll just have to wait and see."

"Let's go to the market after lunch Frank." I said. "Why after lunch." he said. "Well, if I'm not hungry I don't buy so much. Remember that first meal I cooked for you, well, we can pick that up for dinner tonight, how does that sound?" "As a matter of fact," he said, "that sounds like a great idea, what's for lunch?" "It's your turn," I said, "so you tell me, I haven't even had breakfast yet. I think maybe I will have poached eggs this morning, or maybe eggs Benedict, or maybe hash browns and eggs over easy." I was teasing Frank and I could see he knew it. "You know what? I just thought. We didn't have dinner last night, did we?"

he said. I had to think. "No, I guess we didn't." We settled on poached eggs and toast.

After lunch we set out for the market. I always enjoyed going there. People pushing and shoving, waiting in long line ups but the produce was so fresh, it was worth it. We picked up our goodies and remembered we were supposed to stop off at the police station to do the report. It was on the way home so it was no big deal.

"Hello Mrs. Angela." Robert said as we walked into the station. "Do you never get time off Robert? Every time I turn around, you're there." "That's what you get for being a rookie." he said. "Here, I have the forms ready for you and Mr. Bremner." he said. "No, no," I said, "this is Mr. Winston." Frank extended his hand to Robert. "Sorry Mr. Winston." Robert said. "I...." "It's fine Officer," Frank said. "It was an honest mistake. Who wouldn't want to be married to this beautiful woman?" With that he sat down at the desk and started looking over the form. It didn't take long, there was no crime involved.

Robert looked at me. "Did you know Mr. Dodson? He was born here you know, he was 83 but I gather he was bound and determined he would die at sea. I think he would have died happy knowing he got his wish." "You're really an old softy Robert, I said, "and you know what. I have known Hugh for 20 years and I never did know his last name. I feel really bad about that." Frank stood up and reached his hand out to Robert again. "You really have a tough job Officer Robert and we really appreciate all you have done." Robert walked us to the door. "Before I came here I heard things were pretty quiet," Robert said. "Who knew we would have an epidemic. I hope it slows down a bit. I've only been here for a couple of months and already I've been present at an attempted murder, I killed a man, wounded a woman." I interjected. "Oh yes," I said, and of course poor Hugh dying on the boat." "Maybe I should go to the big city." Robert said. "My buddies have had it easier. But then again, I would never have met you Mrs. Angela" He said with a smile. When we got outside, Frank looked at me. "You sure made an impression on Officer Robert Angela, do I have competition?" "Don't be silly," I said. "He's just a boy, but he is cute. I actually feel really sorry for him; he didn't expect to run into so many problems so early in his career. I would hate to be a police officer. They see so many awful things. I just hope Robert keeps some of his warm heart." Frank interrupted my thoughts. "I was picturing Robert a few years from now and hope he remembered how he felt about poor old Hugh."

CHAPTER THIRTY TWO

"Where to now Mrs. Angela, do you have anything else to pick up or are we on our way home?" "No," I said, "I think we have everything we need unless you have any ideas." "Nope, I would really like a nice relaxing day. I have a feeling tomorrow is going to be a challenge. It's cool enough to have a fire isn't it?" He asked. "Sure, why not, I have some logs in the garage. It would be nice to curl up in front of the fire and watch the flames. It really relaxes me."

"We never had a fire place growing up." Frank said, "so I really enjoy them whenever I can." "Where did you live," I asked. "Oh, we lived everywhere. Sometimes for years and other times it was just a month or two." He still didn't answer my question but I didn't press the issue. I wondered if he would ever let me know what his past was. He obviously had had a good education and I felt that he must have spent most of his time in the city but I was only guessing. Or maybe he came from poverty and was embarrassed to talk about it. Too many maybes. I might as well give up trying to guess.

As we walked into the house Franks' phone rang. I was hoping it was Germany calling but he went straight into his bedroom and closed the door. Damn, I hate that. I love a mystery but not when I'm in the middle of it. I thought I could hear him speaking some foreign language but the rooms were fairly sound proof, it just sounded strange. I decided to put the

Tea, Love & Suspicion   97

kettle on. It was my answer to almost everything. I figured I would let Frank figure out which coffee he felt like, there were too many to choose from.

When he walked into the kitchen I tried to figure out if it was a good phone call or a bad one. "Was that your call from Germany?" I asked. "No," he said, "It was Joe from the plant, I'm still hoping they will call but it's a little late for them to call now." He walked out of the kitchen and headed for the living room. Frank had answered my question. I couldn't believe it. I always felt that there were ulterior motives behind everything.

I thought I would start prepping the vegetables and let them soak. The fish wouldn't take long. "Hey Frank," I shouted. "Would you like to bring in some logs from the garage and maybe light the fire?" There was no answer. I walked around the house, knocked on his bedroom door and looked out the front window. Where the heck did he go? I went downstairs and opened the door to the garage. Frank was standing by his car and I could swear I heard it say something. I was really becoming a crazy woman. He closed the car door and asked me if I needed anything. "Yes." I said. "I tried calling you to bring up some logs for the fireplace." "Sure, I'll be up in a minute." "Six should do for the night. I said, and went back up stairs. Cars only talk on television I said to myself, don't be so ridiculous.

The meal was absolutely delicious. We sat at the dining table and had a nice glass of wine to finish off a perfect meal. We put the dishes in the dishwasher and went into the living room to relax. I lit the fire. It was wonderful. I lay down in front of it. I remember when I was a little girl my parents used to burn coal in the fireplace and I would spend hours watching the plumes and different colours that came out of some pieces of coal. The wood I was burning was so dry it was giving off quite a bit of heat. I took my sweater off and lay back down. My undershirt was all I needed.

"Do you mind if I join you?" Frank said. "Please do, it will melt all your cares away." I said. He lay behind me. "Wow, we're spooning." he said as he held me close. We just lay there for the longest time not even saying a word. I could feel his firm body pressed against mine and I felt like I was over- heating. I didn't know if it was the fire or the closeness of Frank. We had never had our bodies so close to each other before and I liked the feeling. He couldn't be gay, could he?

Maybe he thought I had problems and I did in a way but my womanly feelings were definitely intact and I could feel it. I wanted to turn over and make love to him but I bit my lip and stayed very still. He must have been picking up on my thoughts because I could feel a response from him. I couldn't take it any more so I squiggled away from him and stood up. "Would you like a glass of wine Frank?" I said. I think my voice had gone up a pitch and I started for the kitchen. "White or red Frank? If you don't answer, you get white." No answer so I poured him a glass of white. When I came back into the living room he was sitting in front of the fireplace just staring into the flames. I walked towards him with a glass in each hand.

He stood up and grabbed me and kissed me so hard I thought I would suffocate. Then he let me go. I still had the wine glasses in my hands and hadn't spilled a drop. "I think white would be fine," he said and sat back down. Oh boy, I think if the phone hadn't rang, I would have been in trouble.

Saved by the bell I said to myself. It was Jessie. He was having a wonderful time with his grandparents and had gone fishing with his grandpa. "We caught a couple of trout," he said "and they were perfectly delicious. You can't beat fish right out of the lake, especially if you catch them yourself." I could hear my father in the background. "I caught the big one." he said. We had quite a chat, he said he would be coming home at the end of next week and could I pick him up. No problem I said, just e-mail me your flight and time. "Love you too." I said as we hung up.

I turned to Frank and he was fast asleep in front of the fireplace. It's amazing how men can sleep just anywhere I thought. I watched him sleeping. He was such a fine specimen of manhood. Maybe he was wasting his time with me. Maybe he thought that the love I had had for John was still haunting me and he was willing to wait until I was ready. Maybe I should see a shrink. Maybe there was something wrong with me. I'm sure most women would be fighting each other to make love to Frank. I tried to think about what it was that held me back.

I really believed that if I gave him the least bit of encouragement we would be making love every night. I guess I thought if I gave into my feelings he would leave and I didn't want that. I think I must be in love with him or maybe I just loved him. There was a difference I thought. One was much more committed and belonging and the other was more free like the love I had for Jessie. All I wanted for Jessie was the best of what he wanted for himself and he could come and go as he pleased, so long as he kept in touch. Frank was absolutely perfect in every way. Except for one thing. I felt that he wasn't who he appeared to be. I guess that was my biggest problem. How could I get this out of my head? Those hairs on the back of my neck usually meant trouble and I couldn't ignore them.

He turned over and opened his eyes. As I looked into that beautiful face Franks phone dinged. It was his e-mail from Germany. "They're arriving tomorrow at 2pm." he said. "I guess I should get to the office early tomorrow, did you remember to call Mary? I could always drive you to work if you want." "Well, it's a little late to call her now so maybe you could drop me off. I can always have her give me a lift home. What time do you want to leave?" "About 8:00 would be good if that would work for you?" He said. I reached down and grabbed his hand

and helped him off the floor. "You were right," he said, the fire calmed me so much I fell asleep." He hugged me and held me and kissed me good night. I watched him as he headed for the bathroom.

CHAPTER THIRTY THREE

It was just a regular work morning as we both headed into the kitchen but Frank looked particularly handsome this morning. "New suit?" I said. "I love the tie. I always did think charcoal grey suits and yellow ties were so sexy." Frank looked at his tie. "Well, if I'd known that I would have bought more. I didn't like it so much but the sales lady talked me into it." He really did have some nice clothes but men have it easy. One nice suit, lots of different shirts and ties although Frank had quite a few suits to go with them.

As we left for the office Frank was pretty talkative. I think he just couldn't wait to talk to the "guys" from Germany and find out what had happened and was all worked up. He was always so calm. It was nice to see him normal. As he dropped me off at the office, kissed me and told me he would call me as soon as he could and let me know what was going on. "You know I'll be waiting don't you?" I said. "Me too." he said as he waved good-by.

I opened up the office, I was early but I liked it. I loved my staff but I always seemed to get more things done when I came in early. I had no sooner put the coffee on and put the kettle on for my tea when Mary came in. "What are you doing in so early? It's only 20 minutes after 8." Mary reached for the coffee. "I just woke early," she said and thought she might as well get an early start. "By the way, I passed your car on the way in, what's wrong with Frank's car; it's not broken is it?" "No." I said. "He just had to pick up a couple of people from the airport and needs the space."

Mary looked at me. "How was your weekend Angela, did you get lots of rest?" "Well," I said, "it went like this." As I went over the details of what had happened, her eyes got bigger and bigger. "You have got to be kidding." she said. "So did the police arrest that couple?" "No." I said. "They really hadn't done anything wrong. If Frank had signed the contract they could have got them on fraud, I guess. Anyway, I would imagine they are long gone by now." "Poor Hugh." Mary said. "He was a friend of my fathers' so I knew him pretty well years ago. I guess he died as he lived, on a boat." "Oh Mary," I said, "remind me to update our medical supply box and if you would find out who hasn't got their CPR certificate. It's been a while so maybe we can have someone come into the office and get us all at once." "Good idea Angela I'll find out what's a good day for everyone and get them to come in in their sweats, they'd like that."

I broke for lunch and went across the street to the little cafe. I just sat down when Frank walked in. I stood up. "What's wrong?" I said, "No, everything's fine," he said, "I just had to pick up something and when I went into the office they said you were here. What's good to eat? It's your treat." "I'm getting the BLT although the Ruben is good and the tuna melt has always been one of my favourites." "You order," he said, "but nothing sloppy. I don't want to mess up my tie." It was nice that he met me for lunch. He hadn't done that before so no wonder I thought something was wrong. "I phoned the airline before I left and the flight is running about 30 minutes late so I have lots of time." he said.

After lunch I walked him to my car and he set off toward the highway. I thought maybe he wouldn't kiss me good-by, but he did, it was just a little one but we were out in public. As I

Tea, Love & Suspicion   **103**

walked into the office all eyes were on me. "What's up?" I said. "That man of yours Angela," Barbara said, "he must be the most handsome man we have ever seen, even the guys were drooling." Francis piped up. "When I got a flat tire last year all I picked up was a rusty nail." We all laughed. "He is cute though, isn't he?" I said. I could feel my face go red so I retreated into my office.

I picked up the phone and phoned Richard at the marina. "How are you Richard? It's Angela Bremner." "Well, it's been pretty crazy as you can imagine," he said. "I'm trying to get things organized for Hugh's funeral. He had no family and unfortunately no provisions to speak of. I'm not too sure what to do. He knew a lot of people but he never really had any close friends that are still alive." "I would imagine he would have wanted to be cremated and his ashes put in the ocean," I said, "at least that's what I would want. If you could ask around and see if anyone knew what his wishes were and don't worry about any costs, I'll take care of that. Maybe you could contact the funeral parlour and arrange that, just give them my phone number and I will look after it for you." "Oh, that's so kind of you Mrs. Bremner. I was feeling so badly because we have really been suffering financially here for the last year or so. I felt so sorry for you and what you went through yesterday. How are you doing?" he asked. "Well I must admit I've had better days." I said. "I just wish I could have done more for Hugh." We talked for a while and left him with a list of things he should do. After going through Marg.'s death what needed to be done was still fresh in my mind.

CHAPTER THIRTY FOUR

It was 4 o'clock and Frank still hadn't phoned but I wasn't really surprised. I'm sure he was up to his ears. I just hoped things were going well. I had just arranged for Mary to drive me home when Frank walked into the office. I looked into the office and all eyes were on Frank. Poor guy I would imagine he got that all the time. Maybe women were easy for him; I know he certainly didn't think I was. Maybe that was my charm. It was beginning to get a little public in the office so I suggested he tell me what was happening on the way home. "See you tomorrow gang." I said as we left the office. I thought I heard a sigh.

On the way home Frank filled me in on what was going on. Apparently the names of the people Frank had just picked up were the real Winterhoff and Weisinger but Weisinger was a man. It turns out that the impostor Winterhoff was Franz Ilander and was up until recently Vice President in charge of production and sales. He had been fired a few days ago and promised to get even. Weisinger's name was Gerda something or other and was really just his girlfriend along for the ride. He had been involved in all of the negotiations up to the point when he was fired so he knew everything that was happening. "He apparently knew I was staying at the Wycliff, Frank said, "or thought I was." "It was just pure coincidence that we walked into the hotel and he heard Tom call me "Mr. Winston." He took it from there."

"Everything he said made sense and to come in a couple of days early wasn't really unbelievable, so there we are, what a mess." Frank eventually took a breath. "So, what happened to those two impostors?" I said. "Can they do anything to them? Are they back in Germany? Can they charge them with fraud or something?" "Slow down Angela, one question at a time. "First, yes, they are back in Germany and the real Winterhoff had him arrested. I don't know the laws over there but I gather they had him on something. It seems like it was something totally unrelated but he's in jail anyway. I guess they will look into this episode when they get back. Apparently the girlfriend wasn't charged with anything. The good thing is, we are signing the papers tomorrow with my lawyer present. Tonight we will dine. I mentioned 8 o'clock for dinner so they could have some rest, is that fine with you?" "Sounds great." I said. Now, my next problem, what will I wear? People in Germany are always so proper I thought.

I spent quite a long time getting ready; I just wanted to look my best for Frank. These were important guests and I didn't want to let him down. I decided I would let my hair hang loose but I set it in curlers to soften the look. I never wear much makeup but I paid special attention to my eyes. I was lucky, I had good skin I thought. I had decided to wear my green dress, it was a Kelly green and it showed off my blond hair or so I was told by the saleslady. "What's keeping you?" Frank yelled. "I'll be out in 5 minutes." I said. "You have three he shouted back." "Okay, Okay." I said as I gave myself one more look. As I walked out of my room Frank was standing in the doorway. "Vava voom," he said, "you look beautiful." "So do you." I said as I looked him up and down. "Let's go."

As we walked into the hotel, Tom was on the door. "Do you never leave this place?" I said. "Sometimes," he said, "but it was worth working tonight, just to see you. Good evening Mr.

Winston, you lucky man." This was the first time Tom had said anything other than. "Good evening Mr. Winston." Tom gave me a wink and the thumbs up. All of a sudden, I did feel pretty. It was always my older sister that got the looks. She was absolutely gorgeous so I never grew up feeling pretty. As I walked into the restaurant, I even felt taller. Frank took my arm and guided me into the restaurant where Winterhoff and Weisinger were already seated. They both stood up. "I would like to introduce you to Angela Bremner; this is Horst Winterhoff and Frederik Weisinger." "Please to meet you," I said. We were all still standing and I realized they were waiting for me to sit, so I sat. I was really enjoying myself, we were all contributing to the conversation and I didn't feel like I was the odd woman out.

They were charming I thought and so well mannered. I had caught them speaking German when we sat down and although I didn't understand every word, they said that Frank was very lucky to have such a beautiful woman. I just hoped that Frank wouldn't mention the fact that I did speak German because my German was not the same and I didn't know if Frank knew that. As our evening was drawing to a close I excused myself to let the men talk among themselves for a while. As I left, they all stood up. It really made me feel like a woman and it was such a nice way to show respect. Frank was very good and had manners that were somehow lost on some of the younger generation. Not Jessie of course, he knew all the niceties when he was with ladies. I guess it comes from being a single parent, he knew what I felt was proper etiquette. When I came back to the table the men were all standing. I gathered the evening was over. We all said our, pleased to meet you's and Frank and I headed home. He was obviously pleased with how the evening had turned out.

CHAPTER THIRTY FIVE

"Well, I really enjoyed the meal and the company." I said. "I thought I would either be bored or ignored and I felt neither." I was full and happy and I think I did Frank proud. He had headed for his room as soon as we came into the house and came out with a package and already in his sweats. I guess he couldn't get out of his suit fast enough. I headed for my room and intended to do the same thing. "I've put the kettle on for you." he shouted. I never drank tea when I was out because it always tasted like dishwater. I don't think the food industry realizes you have to boil water in order to make tea and at $3 a cup in some places I refused to pay that kind of money.

As I walked into the kitchen I saw a package on my side of the table. "What's this? I said. Frank looked a little embarrassed. "Just a little something I picked up for you when I was away, I forgot to give it to you, sorry." "No need to be sorry," I said, "I didn't know you had anything for me so I haven't been holding my breath, what is it?" "Open it." he said. It wasn't a large package but it wasn't a ring box so whatever it was I liked it already. It was beautifully wrapped in gold paper with a darker gold ribbon tied into a fancy bow. It was almost a shame to open it. Almost, but not quite. As I slowly opened it I could see that Frank was getting a little uncomfortable, so was I. I stopped opening it to make my tea. I thought I would let Frank wait just a little but I couldn't go through with it. I quickly opened the package and saw a beautiful watch. He had been paying attention.

I had been looking through a catalogue a few weeks ago and said how much I really liked the Cartier Santos. It's so elegant and understated I had said. I could have bought it myself but it would have been such a luxury. I looked up at him and I had tears in my eyes. "It's beautiful," I said. I put my arms around him. "You shouldn't have," I said, but I'm glad you did, I love it!" He bent down and kissed me and thanked me for all the things I had done for him. "If only you knew how much I appreciate you Angela, you are the best thing that ever happened to me." I think he was almost in tears because he turned away and pretended to busy himself emptying the dishwasher. "I'll never take it off Frank," I said.

We did our usual thing that evening. We held each other, talked and kissed. I loved it. It was the perfect relationship and thank goodness Frank seemed to know when to back away. I often wondered if it was for my sake or his. Maybe one day I might find out. My bed felt good that night and I was asleep as soon as I lay down.

CHAPTER THIRTY SIX

Frank had already left by the time I got up in the morning and I just decided to go into work a little later. I phoned Mary and told her I would be in around 10 o'clock. That one hour made such a difference. I had woken up early but I just took my time getting ready.

When I walked into my office Mary was right behind me. "How did it go?" she asked. "It was great and much better than I thought it would be." I said. "I felt so happy for Frank. This has been such an ordeal for him. By the way Mary, do you know what time it is?" She looked at my wrist and saw my new watch. "Frank?" She said. "Yes," I said, "isn't it beautiful? He's so sweet Mary but I don't know what to do with him. We are good friends but that's all. Believe it or not." Mary's eyes opened up so wide. "You mean that you haven't?" She couldn't even say it. "No, we haven't," I said. "Oh my God, you've been together for months now, is he Gay?" "I don't know anything anymore," I said, "I think it's me but then again I thought he might be Gay too. This is just between us Mary and I know how hard it will be for you not to confide all of this to Fred, but please don't." "I promise." she said.

"You know Mary, I loved John so much but it's been 14 years and I know John would turn over in his grave if he knew I had been alone for so many years. I just have this feeling in the back of my neck that not everything is as it seems. He only really confided in me this last week about his business and even then I don't really know much. I've never met anybody he works with and he's met pretty well everybody I know. You know Mary, John and I were like two peas in a pod, we shared everything, no secrets and that meant a lot." "Yes, but you grew up with him Angela, you two had the perfect relationship, that rarely ever happens. Frank is his own person and he really seems to care deeply for you, or at least that's what I see."

"When you were in the hospital he was beside himself with worry but couldn't express himself in front of Jessie, even I could see his pain. That being said Angela. If you don't feel right about it, listen to your gut. You're a smart woman Angela you'll know soon enough." The phone rang and we both got back to work.

It was Richard from the marina. He had planned everything. His wife Freda had helped with the organizing and it was just a case of paying for the services and the eulogy. They would have it on board one of the boats and sprinkle his ashes on the outgoing tide. I thought that was a great idea. He didn't have many friends but those he did have were all associated with the sea. "Please ask Freda to get the invoices to me," I said, and I will take care of things. What day are you planning for the eulogy? Friday would be fine, I'll be there but have Freda call me on Thursday so we can make sure that everything has been done and thank Freda for me."

CHAPTER THIRTY SEVEN

I got home a little later than usual and the house was so quiet I couldn't stand it. I used to know when Frank was home but since he parked his car in the garage I couldn't tell. I shouted to see if anyone answered and nobody did. I went up to my room and changed. I just put the kettle on when the phone rang. "Jessie, how are you doing?" I said. We must have talked for 45 minutes or should I say he did. He had been fishing almost every day and said that his grandmother was the best cook ever. My parents loved to see Jessie he was so much fun for them and they loved spoiling him. He was the son they never had and I think it made them feel young again. Jessie told me that my sister Alice was living in the South of France. I was glad she was in France and hope she stayed there. I really wouldn't like her to meet Frank. She was more than a flirt and had tried to take John away from me many times. She didn't know it but John really didn't like her. She made my life miserable growing up.

Jessie said he would be home on Saturday and wondered if I was driving Frank's car yet. I told him there wasn't room for his suitcase and I had no intention of driving it anyway. I liked my own car. Jessie would only be home for a few days and then he was on his way back to school. I wish I had had more time with him but with all that had been happening here I was glad he hadn't been here.

I put one of my frozen chicken pies in the oven and prepared some vegetables, it was almost 7 o'clock and Frank hadn't come home. I wasn't sure what time his guests were leaving but he couldn't have taken them in his car so maybe he got a rental. I had such a good imagination I thought. I was always trying to figure things out before they happened. I was usually wrong. It's possible he went into the city it was only a half hour drive from the airport. I was going to have to stop thinking, I drove myself crazy.

I sat at the kitchen table eating my dinner when I heard Franks' car drive into the garage. "Did you miss me?" he said as he bent down to kiss me. "No, I've been too busy, did you eat yet?" "Yes," he said, "sorry, I should have phoned you." "Did you get Winterhoff and Weisinger on their flight?" I asked. "Oh yes," Frank said, "I was so glad when they left." They were really nice but I don't like the PR side of the business. I'm not very good at it." "Do you mind if I light the fire Angela? It just feels so good and there won't be too many more cool nights and I need to relax." "Go ahead," I said, "you know where everything is." "I'll go get changed and by that time you'll be ready to join me, right?" "Sure." I said.

Then I thought of last night and how close we came to making love. I thought about my conversation with Mary and how my doubts kept me from letting go. I finished my dinner and cleared the table. I could hear Frank cussing at the fire. He couldn't get it to light so I went into the living room to help him. "Did you use kindling?" I asked. "What's kindling?" He said. "I have some beside the logs, there just small pieces of wood, it makes it easier to light." "I'll get it." He said, and marched off down to the garage. He came back with a few pieces. "You weren't a boy scout were you Frank?" "Nope," he said, "but I think I just earned my badge." "There!" he said with such pride. "I just lit my first fire." I must admit it felt wonderful to sit in

Tea, Love & Suspicion   **113**

front of a roaring fire although I had to back off a little, I was getting too warm. I got up onto my knees and Frank sat up beside me. We were face to face. He was so tall we rarely got to be eye to eye, I liked it. Frank shuffled over to me and pulled me towards him.

We both fell over. I felt his hand on my breast but only for a moment. We rolled over and over and kissed so passionately I thought I would explode. I could feel that Frank was having the same problem. He was the one to back off this time, although I was so glad he did. "Want some wine?" he said as he walked into the kitchen. "White or red?" "Your choice." I lay on my stomach with my face in a pillow. I lifted my face out of the pillow. "White." I said. I wasn't too sure how much more I could take or how much he could take either. I was at the point that I didn't know if it was him or me that was stopping us from making love. We came so close last night and I was the one who went for the wine. Tonight, it was Frank. I think I will hide the firewood. I decided I would have to change the mood.

"What happens now?" I said. "Now that you've signed the contract with W&W." My short form for Winterhoff and Weisinger." "Nothing till next week, there's still lots to do before we start production. I think I will sleep late tomorrow" Frank said, "I've had one hell of a few days and my Assistant can take care of things for a change." A day without meetings that's a first I thought. "Oh, by the way," I said, "their having a eulogy for Hugh on Friday at the marina, did you want to come? You really didn't know him so it would be fine if you decided not to." "No, I'll come with you." he said. "And, Jessie is coming home on Saturday. Things don't seem to slow down, do they?" I said. "Nope." he said. "I'm sure glad it's a holiday weekend."

CHAPTER THIRTY EIGHT

The eulogy for Hugh was wonderful. They had decorated the boat with pictures of Hugh through the years. There were even pictures of John and me with Hugh. It took me back to the days when we felt so free and happy. Frank saw me looking at the pictures. "You look like you were about 10 years old in that one." he said. "Is that John?" "Yes," I said, that's John." "He really was handsome." Frank said. "Yes, I said, he sure was." I was feeling a little melancholy. It was funny, John was very handsome and so was Frank but they were completely different. Frank had a sturdy athletic build more like a middle weight boxer, but taller and John was more like a long distance swimmer.

I was drifting off remembering. All of us so young and healthy in those days without a care in the world. "Thank you for the good times Hugh." I said out loud. I thanked Freda and Richard for taking care of things. Richard shook my hand. "We wouldn't have been able to do this if it hadn't been for you Mrs. Bremner. We just couldn't have afforded such a great send off and I am sure that Hugh would have loved to be here with us." "He is." I said.

I met some of the people I had known when John was alive and it was nice to reminisce. We were just pulling up to the dock, our tribute to Hugh was done and his ashes were floating on the ocean. It was 2 o'clock by the time we reached the dock. We all had to get back to work. He drove Mary and me back to

Tea, Love & Suspicion

the office. "I'll see you later." he said as he drove off. He didn't kiss me. That was the first time since I had met him that he didn't either kiss me hello, good-by or goodnight. Was it because Mary was there or was the picture of John the last straw?

CHAPTER THIRTY NINE

I was home a little earlier than usual. It would seem that my team in the office had taken care of all the important stuff and we all left early, it was Friday and the beginning of a long weekend. As I walked through my front door I was thinking about what I was going to make for dinner when I heard Frank shouting again in that foreign language. He saw me and looked surprise and indicated he'd only be 2 minutes, turned and went into his bedroom. It wouldn't have made any difference if he'd stayed in the living room, I didn't understand a word he said anyway. Although the last time I heard him talking like that I had made a mental note of the couple of words I could make out.

When I Googled it, it seemed like it was Arabic but it could have been Romanian for all I knew. Why didn't I just ask him instead of putting myself through these cloak and dagger scenarios? When he came out of his room, he was his usual cheerful self. Then I remembered how in some languages it sounds much worse than it is. I remembered one time when I was in Italy and I thought the couple at the B&B were going to kill each other, their arms were flailing around and their voices were raised. I found out later they weren't angry with each other at all, it just sounded that way.

As Frank came into the kitchen, he kissed me on the cheek and said he had already picked up something for dinner. Pre-made lasagne. It turned out really well. "Where did you get this from?" I asked. He looked quite proud of himself. "In town next to the bakery," he said, "they have meat pies and all sorts of stuff. I've been there a few times for lunch and no matter what I had, it always tasted good." "I'll have to remember that," I said, "it was good."

"Oh, by the way Frank, are you coming with me tomorrow to pick up Jessie, his flight arrives at 11am." "Sure," he said, "we can stop off at the market and pick up some seafood, I've been craving shrimp and crab and salad. Does that sound like a plan?" Jessie and I both loved sea food so it sounded like a fantastic idea. I always looked forward to going to the market, even though I always seem to buy more than I needed.

Jessie's flight was right on time. As he came towards us I noticed how much he looked like his father. Although I thought he could use a haircut. His hair was dark brown and wavy, just like John's was. He was such a handsome boy although he certainly wasn't a boy anymore. He had grown so tall, only a couple of inches shorter than Frank. We hugged and kissed each other and then he turned to Frank. They shook hands and bumped shoulders, definitely a guy thing. "Good to see you Frank. Mum was saying that you've been working petty hard but she likes your cooking." "Ha Ha," Frank said, "I doubt that."

On the way into town Jessie didn't stop talking, he had had such a good time with his grandparents. Jessie was an old soul so he felt very comfortable with older people. He actually went with his grandmother to bingo. I can just picture him talking to all the old folk. I turned to Jessie. "Frank mentioned stopping in at the market for some sea food." "Great idea," Jessie said, "I've had lots of trout but shrimp, scallops and crab sounds awesome." As we wandered around the marketplace I thought how much we looked like a family. I had to stop thinking. I think I will have to write that down 200 times before I get it through my head that I have to stop elaborating on things. We ended up with three bags of goodies and headed home.

CHAPTER FORTY

As soon as we got home Frank started preparing the sea food. It was like he had done it many times before. Maybe he grew up on the coast somewhere or maybe he had cooked this meal for others. I watched him as he was cooking and he looked quite comfortable, especially with this meal. I had watched him at other times and he always looked awkward. Maybe this was a special family meal. I wonder what his family was like. There I go again. I have to stop the thinking. Jessie was washing the lettuce and preparing the things for our salad. We had everything including the kitchen sink. Apple, carrot, raisins, nuts, broccoli, sugar peas, spinach, butter lettuce and the list went on and I was salivating. I really didn't have to do much of anything, it was all under control. Actually, I got the buns out, set the table and made the salad dressing, my contribution. As we sat down at the dining table I thought of us again, as a family. The meal was fantastic and we had enough sea food left over to have it in pasta the next day. Happiness is I thought.

"By the way Jessie." I said. "I booked your flight for Thursday at 2 pm, is that good for you?" "That's great mum, thanks. I was thinking, he said, of going over to see Barry tomorrow, I guess I won't see him for a while, would that be okay and can I borrow your car?" I looked at Frank, he nodded. I gathered that Frank didn't have too much to do tomorrow and could take me if I needed to. "Sure, that's fine. I don't have anything planned for tomorrow." I said. Jessie had had a car before he left for university but had sold it and he was lost without it. It just didn't make any sense paying insurance if he wasn't here to use it.

Most of his friends lived quite a way from us and the bus service sucked, his words, not mine. Not only that, he liked driving my new BMW. My thoughts were interrupted when I thought I could hear someone talking.

I got up from the table and wandered around the house trying to find out where the voice was coming from. It sounded like a radio. As I got closer to the stairs to the garage, it got louder. "Frank, come here!" I shouted. He came over to me. "Can you hear that?" "Oh, yes." he said. "That's my car. It does its own diagnostics and lets me know what's going on." "That scared the you know what out of me Frank Winston." I said. "I thought there was someone in the house." He put his arms around me and told me he was sorry. "It doesn't do it very often." he said, but he guessed he should have warned me. Jessie was watching us and I backed away from Frank. Jessie just raised his eyebrows and smiled. I'm sure Jessie wasn't a virgin so I am sure he thought there was more going on than there was. Either way, it didn't matter. I knew.

Jessie was about to light the fire when Frank spoke up. "Let me do it Jessie, I have to light two fires, on my own, successfully, then I get my merit badge." "You're what?" Jessie said as he looked at me. "It's a long story," I said, "just let him do it, he needs the practice."

Before long the fire was roaring. I had gone into my room and had made up a paper badge with Boy Scout Merit Badge and underneath I wrote: "Frank Winston has successfully lit two fires and is now considered the permanent fire lighter". I looked into my stereo collection and found Jose Feliciano's "Light my Fire" album and put it on. Frank was sitting by the fire when it started playing. "Get up," I said. "Now, stand straight and

Tea, Love & Suspicion **121**

give the Boy Scout salute." Jessie had to help him with that. As the stereo played "Light my Fire." I presented him with the paper I had written up for him and tapped him on the shoulder. "Congratulations Mr. Winston," I said, you now have your fire lighting patch." Jessie saluted him and we all laughed. "I'll keep this forever." He said. It was like we were on automatic, he hugged me and kissed me on the lips and Jessie didn't seem to flinch.

"Let's play Scrabble," Jessie said and maybe you can get your spelling badge Frank." "One badge per nights all I'm allowed Jessie but I would love to play Scrabble." We played until midnight, Jessie won, he always did. Frank and I came in a close second. "I think it's time for bed." I said and we all set off in our different directions. Once Jessie was downstairs Frank and I met in the middle of the hallway and he gave me my goodnight kiss. We had had a wonderful day.

CHAPTER FORTY ONE

Sunday really was a day of rest. Neither Frank nor I felt very energetic. He stayed in his room until noon. He said he felt like reading a book and taking it easy. I think I might come out for lunch he had said and as always he was on time.

At 12 o'clock he came out of his room and headed for the kitchen. I was eating my lunch. I had already made a soup out of some of the vegetables we had had last night and it tasted pretty good. He kissed me on the top of the head and put his coffee on. Just then his phone rang and he headed back into his bedroom. When he came back into the kitchen he had a strange look on his face. "That was my sister." he said. "Who?" I said, "I didn't even know you had a sister." "Well, she was on her way to Australia and she wanted to stop here to see me. I told her I would pick her up at the airport and she could stay overnight at the hotel." "When is she coming?" I asked. "Tomorrow." "Wow, that's short notice," I said, "what time?" "It's an early flight so she should be arriving around 10 o'clock. I was thinking maybe you could meet her later, how about over dinner? I'll check with Tara when I pick her up." "Is she younger or older than you?" I asked. "She's a couple of years younger than me but she's bossy and thinks she can tell me what to do. You'll know when you meet her." I couldn't wait. Maybe I could learn more from her about who Frank was.

Tea, Love & Suspicion   123

Jessie phoned later that day to ask if it was alright that he stayed the night at Barry's house. "No problem," I said, but Frank's sister is coming into town tomorrow so I might need my car later in the day." "I'll be back around 1 o'clock," Jessie said, "would that be fine with you?" "Yes, no problem," I said. Frank wants me to meet his sister so I would imagine it would be for dinner, I'll know more tomorrow." "Okay Mum, I'll call you in the morning no doubt James will have me awake early anyway. He's so cute Mum, you would love him." "Okay Jessie, give me a call tomorrow."

Frank was pretty quiet that night, we watched TV and he didn't even hint about having a fire. Frank had had a lot happening lately but it would seem that after his sister's call he was even more withdrawn. It seemed like he was really trying to be light hearted for me, but I felt the difference. I couldn't wait to meet her.

"I'll leave around 9am." he said. I think her luggage is going straight through so she doesn't have to wait for it." "You don't seem too thrilled that you're going to see her Frank, do you not get along with her?" "If I had known that my sister was coming here, I wouldn't have answered her call. We have nothing in common and I can't even say I like her." "I know what you mean," I said, "I always used to say, you can pick your friends but you can't pick your relatives and it's so true." "Yes," he said, "I guess that is true."

He was gone the next day before I got up so I would wait for his phone call. I looked through my closet to find out what I should wear. I decided on what I called a dressy pant suit. I had bought it in New York last year at Versace and it had cost me a fortune. It was just one of those very extravagant things you impulsively buy but don't wear. I tried it on and it really looked fantastic.

I guess I really hadn't gone out much before Frank came into my life so it had just sat there. I had just put my hair up when he phoned. "How about I pick you up around 6 o'clock?" He said. "Sure, that would be fine, would you rather I took my car and met you there." "No," he said, "I'll pick you up." I had no sooner put the phone down and it rang again, it was Jessie.

"I'll be home around 4 o'clock mum will that are good for you?" "I plan on spending the night at home so the car is all yours." "Don't worry about it, Frank is picking me up," I said, "so I don't really need it but I'll see you before I leave. Frank's sister is staying at the hotel so he wanted to pick me up rather than have me take my own car." "Thanks mum, I'll see you later." Jessie said.

I was feeling really nervous about meeting Frank's sister and I tried to picture what she looked like. I know my sister Alice was really beautiful. I was always told that I had a quiet beauty but my sisters screamed. I wonder if Tara was like that. Frank was incredibly good looking but he was never full of himself, in fact it seemed that he was totally unaware of his good looks. I would just have to wait and see.

CHAPTER FORTY TWO

Frank was true to his word, he was coming through the door at 6 on the dot, and I was ready to leave. "You look great," he said, "is that a new outfit?" "Yes and no," I said, "I just haven't worn it before. Does it look okay?" "You bet," he said, but you always look great, right Jessie?" "Hot." Jessie said. He rarely saw me dressed up. I had always been a home body so even he was impressed. "Now, I'm ready for anything." I said. "Let's go."

When we walked into the restaurant I saw this most gorgeous woman sitting at the bar. Oh my, I thought, it's my sister Alice. It wasn't of course but she was just as beautiful. I wondered how he was going to introduce me. This is my landlady, this is my friend, this is my companion. I really didn't expect he would call me his girl-friend, so I waited. "Tara, I would like you to meet Angela." That was easy I thought. "I'm so glad to meet you, and you look so beautiful." She said as she looked back at Frank. He looked a little uncomfortable and I felt the hairs stand up on my neck. Oh no, I thought, not again.

As it happens our dinner time was almost pleasant. She was asking all kinds of questions about the area, did I have children, was I married and I was getting a little defensive. "I'm a widow, I said and I have one son." "I'm so sorry." she said. I wasn't sure if she was talking about my late husband or my son. I always said, it's not what you say, it's how you say it and Tara had a way with words. Frank hardly said a word, he definitely looked uncomfortable but I could relate to that because of my sister.

It was about 9:30 when Frank said to Tara that she must be getting pretty tired and suggested he meet her tomorrow for breakfast around 9 o'clock. "What time is your flight again?" he asked. "Not till 12:30." she replied. "I will bid you goodnight Angela, it was so good to meet you and I hope we will meet again someday." she said although I didn't think she meant it. I replied with the same pleasantries and Frank and I left for home. Neither of us talked on the drive home.

CHAPTER FORTY THREE

It was midnight and I was already in bed when I heard a loud knock on my door. I sat straight up in bed. It was Frank. "What's wrong?" I said. Frank looked a little upset. It was Tara, she had fallen and thought she might have a broken her ankle. I was wondering what the heck she was doing up at this time, I thought she had gone to bed. She had apparently slipped in the shower. "I better go see what's up," he said. "I just wanted you to know what was going on." Jessie had come upstairs to get a drink and was talking to Frank so I went back to bed. There was nothing I could do. Instinctively I didn't really like her but I hoped she would be okay so she wouldn't have to delay her trip.

When I got up in the morning I had my shower and went into the kitchen to put the kettle on. I thought I would check and see if Franks' car was in the garage to see if he had made it home. It was only 7:30 so if he did come home he wouldn't have left that early to see Tara for breakfast. The garage was empty. I peeked into Jessie's room and he was fast asleep so I went upstairs to have my breakfast. I was so glad I had decided to take extra days off while Jessie was home, no panic.

It was 11:30 by the time Jessie came upstairs. "What a night." he said. "Why? What happened?" I asked. Jessie filled me in on what had happened. Frank had asked him to follow him to the hotel. He didn't want to have to take Tara to the hospital if it wasn't necessary. He said that his sister was leaving in the morning on her trip and she really couldn't miss her flight. "She was lucky mum. She really did hurt herself but nothing was broken, just a really bad sprain. I'm glad I had taken our medical supply box with me because when I applied the tenser bandage to her ankle, it seemed to help. I told her to get it checked when she got where she was going and to elevate it as much as she could on the flight."

"Apparently she had pain medication Jessie said. "I'm assuming she is now on her way to Russia." "Russia?" I said, "I thought she was going to Australia." Jessie looked at me. "Well I saw her itinerary on the coffee table and it was a one way to Russia. I didn't intend to be nosey but it was just sitting in front of me." Apparently Frank had gone downstairs to the front desk to see if he could get a glass of milk for Tara to take her meds. She was in the bathroom soaking her ankle in the tub. "She's quite a looker mum, she reminds me of Aunt Alice." "I know what you mean," I said. "I was already binding her ankle when Frank came up with her milk and I left as soon as I was finished and that was it Jessie said. I came home."

"She was a little weird mum and who needs another Alice around. She kissed my hand as I left and said that she was sure we would meet again." With that he went back downstairs to have a shower. Obviously her beauty didn't impress him. I have a smart boy, I thought. I just hoped that his mother was just as smart. Eventually Frank came home and he looked exhausted. "Well, she's on her way to Australia. It's a long trip so I hope she's not in too much pain. I need a coffee really badly." He said. He had obviously spent the night at the hotel. I wondered if she had lied about her destination to Frank or Frank wasn't telling me the truth. "Why is she going to Australia?" I asked. "It's something to do with her company and she has friends over there." he said. Now I was really suspicious and the hairs on my neck were working overtime but what could I do, or say. Frank didn't know that Jessie had seen her airline ticket. If she hadn't hurt her ankle I would never have been the wiser.

CHAPTER FORTY FOUR

I wasn't sure how much more of this cloak and dagger life I could take. My life had always been so organized and uncomplicated. Frank had turned my life upside down but I was so in love I couldn't see straight when it came to him. So far it was only my suspicions based on no true facts that were plaguing me. Or was I forever making excuses for him? When I came into the kitchen he had already made his coffee and was standing leaning against the counter. I thought that if he moved, he would have fallen over.

"Come over here." he said. I walked over to him. He put his coffee down and put his arms around me. "I'm so tired." He said. "You're the only thing in my life that makes any sense." He kissed me and held me. I think he needed me now more than I needed him so I held him until he let go. "I think I will go to bed." he said. I thought that would be a good idea. I told him I would wake him for dinner. I didn't bother to wake him until dinner was almost ready.

I knocked on his door. I think he must have been awake already. "I'll be out in a minute," he said. Jessie was still in his room so I let him know that dinner would be in 5 minutes if he wanted to eat. The sea food pasta was great although we all seemed pre-occupied with our own thoughts and it was obvious. Frank was the first one to break the silence. "How about we go to a movie tonight? Does anyone know what's on?" Jessie said he was going out with his friends for a farewell get together so he couldn't make it and I was now the one that was tired. I mustered up the energy to phone the theatre but there was nothing really interesting so we decided to stay in and watch TV.

Jessie slept all day Wednesday while I caught up on some paper work Mary had brought over for me. He started to pack that evening so he wouldn't be pressured before his flight. I thought he might have to take another suitcase he had so much stuff he wanted to take back with him but he managed to get it all in. His day to leave came too quickly and I knew I would miss him.

Jessie and Frank said their goodbyes and did that hand shake and bump shoulder thing. "I know you'll do well Jessie and don't forget to keep in touch with your mother, she's going to miss you you know." Frank said. Jessie smiled, "Yes, I hate to leave but I'm looking forward to getting back to the studies, go figure." he said. We all left at the same time, Frank asked me if I was going to work after I had dropped Jessie off, I said I was and that I would be home around 5. He actually gave me a little kiss and told me to drive safe. "You too." I said.

I felt terrible seeing Jessie leave on the plane. It would be a long time before he could get back for another visit. I knew I was going to miss him terribly but at least I had Frank to keep me company. As I drove off to the office I remembered I needed to pick up some papers that I had been working on so I swung by the house.

Franks' car was in the garage and the door was open. It looked like he was loading something into his car. I just walked in as the car door closed. Frank saw me and noticeably jumped. "You scared me," he said. I thought you were at work." "I thought you were too." I said. Frank looked a little uncomfortable. "What did you forget? He said. "Oh I forget to take some papers with me and I need them this afternoon. What's your excuse? I said. "Oh, I just wanted to take some clothes to the dry cleaner I have so many suits and they all seem like they need help." he said. I passed by him and went upstairs to collect my papers. When I came back down he was waiting for me. "I'll be home early tonight." He said. "Do you want me to pick anything up?" "Not that I can think of but if you think of something for dinner, that would be nice." I said. "Sounds good." He said as he climbed into his car.

CHAPTER FORTY FIVE

Frank was already home by the time I got there and had started to make dinner. "I bought some steaks and I've put the potatoes in the oven. Dinner should be ready in about half an hour," he said, "are you hungry?" "Hungry enough." I said as I put the kettle on. He pinched my bottom and said he was sorry that things had been so messed up lately. I hugged him and told him everything would work out for the best. He said, "I hope so." and turned away. We certainly seemed to base our life on food and sleep, the necessities of life I thought.

Frank had already set the dinner table and put wine glasses out. He sure went all out tonight I thought, it was great and I was going to make the most of it. The steak was perfect but although the potatoes were good, they could have stayed in the oven a little longer but with lots of butter, salt and pepper, they were just fine. By the time we put the dishes in the dishwasher it was 6 o'clock and we settled down to watch TV.

I was feeling better and Frank was back to normal. Hugging and kissing and it felt wonderful. I got up to go to the kitchen and turned around to say something. Frank was right behind me and I was two steps up on the landing. We were eye to eye. I looked into those green eyes and melted. I put my arms around him and kissed him hard. He responded with more than I was expecting. He picked me up and took me into my bedroom. I didn't resist.

CHAPTER FORTY SIX

By the time we got into the bedroom we were like two wild animals. Neither of us could control the urge. It was like the beginning of a volcanic explosion. I had never felt such lack of control. As he threw me on the bed I was helpless. He looked at me, undressed me and kissed every part of my body. I could feel myself rolling in ecstasy as his hands caressed my breasts. I wanted him now and I pulled him on top of me. "Slowly." he said, but I couldn't wait any longer and I guided him towards me. The moment our bodies came together there was no stopping. I was in another world. His athletic body glistened in the failing light and we made love like nothing I have ever felt before. He was the master of my body. I never knew there were so many ways to make love. It felt like a ballet. Every move he made I followed, willingly. As we eventually lay side by side we were both out of breath. "Why now?" I said. "For a couple of reasons, but most of all, it was your kiss." He said as he smiled at me.

"Tonight was the very first time, you kissed me." Frank said. "I was waiting for you to want me as much as I wanted you. I could have made love to you the very first day I met you. I remember you in the car with the window open about 3 inches, afraid that I was some kind of monster. For me, it was love at first sight. As time went on and I got to know you, I realized that you were still holding old memories. I couldn't compete with that. I never knew I could feel like this about anyone Angela." he said. "I love you, more than you will ever know." He kissed me tenderly and said. "Don't ever forget it."

We made mad passionate love all night and each time became more sensual that before, we were sticking together from the sweat, we were sliding back and forward on each other's bodies till we just couldn't take it anymore. "I need water and a shower," he said, "how about you?" "Both," I said, "shower first." With that he took me into his arms and into my bathroom. "Wow," he said, "you could have a party in here." I had had Jack put a huge shower in my en-suit with water coming from every direction, even from the ceiling. As we turned the water on we were pummelled from all sides. He picked up the soap and washed me from head to toe and I stood there enjoying every moment and I was ready to make love again. He needed some encouragement. I took the soap from him and washed his beautiful body. His body was firm and he stood there with water running down him from all sides and I caressed him. He picked me up and our love making started again. I didn't think it was possible to make love so many times, but we did. We let the water flow over our bodies until we eventually parted.

After we dried off and drank what seemed to be a bucket of water we lay back down on the bed. It was still early but we had been making love for hours, it seemed like we couldn't get enough of each other. I thought our night of love making was over and I turned away from him. "Oh no you don't." he said as he turned me back and kissed me. He enveloped me in his arms and held me tight. I thought he was going to break me. I could see tears rolling down his cheek as he held me. "I've never felt like this before," he said, "and I don't know what to do." "You know I love you, don't you Frank?" I said. "I tried so hard to keep you at a distance but all the time my love for you was growing. I don't know what I would do without you." He sat straight up. "Don't say that Angela, you know no matter what, you're a survivor." He kissed me so hard I could hardly breathe. We eventually drifted off to sleep.

CHAPTER FORTY SEVEN

When I woke up my body was aching. I turned to see Frank but he was already out of bed. I had another quick shower, threw my robe on and went into the kitchen to put the kettle on. "Frank, where are you?" I shouted. There was no reply. The door to his room had always been closed but it wasn't this morning. I peeked in and called his name, no answer but I could see that the bed was still made up. I decided to check to see if his car was there, it was, where the hell could he be? I walked into his room and it was as if nobody lived in it. Nothing was out of place, now that's creepy, I thought, nobody is that neat. I walked over to his walk-in closet. As I opened it, I panicked. It was empty. "No! I screamed, "NO!" I raced over to check the dresser drawers. They were empty except for one small white piece of paper with two green contact lenses on it. Oh my God I said to myself as I fell to the floor, this can't be happening. Not now. "WHY!" I screamed as I crumpled into a ball on the floor and wept till I could weep no more. I eventually got up and ripped his bed apart, cursing his name. Paper fell from the sheets with writing on it. "Remember," it said, "I will always love you and don't ever forget it." Why would he have hidden the note, maybe he had been abducted. I was tired of maybes I needed to talk to him now.

I ran to the kitchen to find my phone and called Franks' cell, his lifeline I called it. I'm sorry said the recording, this number is no longer in service, my heart dropped. I'll call the plant they must know where he is. I got the same recording, no longer in service. I felt like dying. I had to have some tea and think. As I sat at the kitchen table I thought how little I knew of him and now, I knew even less. No green eyes, I'm sure it wasn't even his real name either. His so called sister was really the only person connected to him that I had met and now I doubted that she wasn't even his sister. Maybe he ran away with her. Except for Winterhoff and Weisinger, they were the only people I knew that knew Frank.

As I sat wondering what to do, I thought back to last night and the mad passionate love we had made, was it real? Oh yes it was. All of a sudden my heart skipped a beat. We hadn't used any protection. John and I had never used protection, we always wanted more children but it just wasn't meant to be. Birth control pills were out of the question. I hadn't had sex for 14 years. I had to think. Oh my God, how stupid I'd been and I didn't have a clue what I should do now. I rushed over to my computer, I was sure I would find the answer there.

CHAPTER FORTY EIGHT

I had heard of the morning after pill so I looked it up. It wasn't fool proof although it had an incredibly high rate of success. I had to try it. There were pregnancy testers that you could do at home so I should get a couple of them. I couldn't go to our local Pharmacy, I'd known old Mike for years, I would have to go into the city. My eyes were so red and puffy I thought I should put an ice pack on my face for a while before I tried to put my makeup on. I couldn't stand the thoughts of going into my bedroom just yet so I lay on the sofa for a couple of minutes wondering what to do next.

I suddenly realized that I really couldn't waste any time so I made myself get ready. As I looked through my closet I chose my black jacket and remembered it was the one I wore the day Margaret died. Could this day get any worse I thought, then I noticed the letter Marg. had left for me. I had forgotten all about it. I just hoped there were no last minute requests in it. I opened up the envelope and read it.

"My dearest Angela, if you are reading this letter it means I am no longer on this planet. I have a confession to make. About 61 years ago I was engaged to a wonderful boy, Bill. I loved him so much but two weeks before we were married he was killed in a car accident. I thought I would never recover and in a way I didn't. I found out I was pregnant with his child. In those days that was probably the worst sin, not only for me but for my whole family. By the time I started to show my parents sent me away, to college they said. My older sister Nettie had been married for 6 years and they were childless, so, it was decided that my sister Nettie would pretend to be pregnant and when the time came she would come to me and I would hand over my baby. I'm not sure if you remember them as both Nettie and her husband died very young. Now you know why I have been so close to Gail and why I am leaving everything I have to her and her husband. I forever regret that I never told Gail I was her mother but I was sworn to take my secret to the grave. My request to you is that when the time is right, take Gail aside and tell her. I have forever and always regretted the fact that I didn't have the chance to raise her as my own, as good as the arrangement was, I always felt like I was on the outside looking in. If things had been like they are now, I would have raised her myself and to hell with the gossip.

And, by the way. The twenty thousand I had in my freezer is half for you to take that man of yours on a holiday and the other half is for Jessie when he graduates. The beef in the freezer is also for you and anyone who wants to eat it. Goodbye my best friend, I will miss you.

Love & tea breaks, Margaret."

I couldn't believe what I had just read. My best friend was there for me even beyond the grave and at that moment I knew what I had to do. If the morning after pills didn't work and I had become pregnant, I would keep the baby. I had only just turned 38 and lots of women were just having their first child at that age. I would have to leave it up the fates. I wondered what Jessie would think but after reading Marg.'s letter I knew I was the only one to make that decision. Besides, Jessie loved kids, I think. Damn that Frank, I was now just angry with him for leaving me with this decision. The thought that he may never come back made me feel ill.

CHAPTER FORTY NINE

I climbed into my car and headed for the city. The freeway was almost empty except for myself and someone else heading in the same direction. As I got to the outskirts of the city I saw a pharmacy and pulled into the parking lot. There was nobody in the store, thank goodness so I felt free to look around and see if I could find what I was looking for without having to ask. Just then a man came into the store and went straight to the magazine section. He was bent down looking through the magazines.

I really didn't know what the best product was so I thought I might as well ask the pharmacist. I quietly asked him about the pills, the pregnancy testers and condoms. I never knew there were so many types of condoms, sizes, types, raspberry and the list went on. I told him we were having a sex education program for adults. He nodded his head. "Good thing," he said, "they should have started that years ago. The only trouble is, the morning after pills I have need a prescription but I am sure the Pharmacy in the mall have the ones you can buy over the counter." I thanked him and paid for the condoms and the testers.

As I walked over to my car I noticed that the car that had been behind me on the freeway was also parked in the lot, it wasn't hard to notice, there were only three cars in the lot and that included mine. I was getting paranoid again. I got into my car and drove over to the mall and parked. As I looked behind me I saw that same car parking about 6 stalls over from me. I decided I would walk nonchalantly towards it. Before I got to see who was in the car it backed out of the stall and took off towards the road. Could that be Frank? No, it must have been that man in the pharmacy. It was just a co-incidence I told myself, I had to stop making things more than they were. I picked up my pill from the Pharmacy and headed home. I was keeping an eye on my rear view mirror but nobody followed and I relaxed. When I got home, I took the pill.

CHAPTER FIFTY

The days passed but the nights were long. I cried myself to sleep every night and my eyes were always red. I had used up the pregnancy testers and they both showed positive and the morning sickness was starting to be an all-day thing. Obviously I was the one in a million where the morning after pill didn't work. This baby was bound and determined it was going to be born. Instead of gaining weight, I was losing it. I was still having my morning tea with Mary and without warning she said, "Are you pregnant?" I looked away as the tears welled up in my eyes. "How long will Frank be away?" she asked. I had told everyone that Frank had been called away on a secret mission and we hadn't talked since he left. Everybody seemed to accept the explanation. Some I am sure thought he might be dead but they never voiced their thoughts.

I was becoming a good liar, much to my chagrin. I had learned from the best I thought. I didn't tell Mary anything different about Frank's disappearance but I did confirm the fact that I was pregnant. "What are you going to do?" she said. "Keep it of course." I said. "I never believed in abortion for myself although I do understand why people are driven to it. I have enough money, I'm young enough and I couldn't dream of terminating my pregnancy now. We only had sex the night before he left." I said, "I guess it was meant to be." I knew I wouldn't be able to keep it a secret for long but for now I asked Mary to keep it to herself.

The weeks passed and I started to blossom. I had to make it known to the office staff and surprisingly they were happy for me. I had met with Gail after I had read Marg.'s letter and she had broken down in tears as she read her mother's letter. "I wish she had told me," Gail said, "I always did feel a bond with her that I couldn't explain. Now I know why." I told her about my condition and she hugged me and told me how lucky any child would be to have me as their mother. As far as she was concerned I was doing the right thing.

She promised to keep the information to herself and as far as I know, she did. It was going to be pretty obvious before long anyway she had said, so I only have to keep quiet for a couple more months, right? That was Gail. I think she felt privileged that she was the first to know.

CHAPTER FIFTY ONE

Weeks turned into months and I was watching the ultrasound. "I can't make out which end is which." I said. "I can," the Doctor said, "you're going to be the proud mother of twins." I almost fell off the table. "Boys or girls?" I said. "No, please, don't tell me, I don't want to know, I'll find out when they're born." Once I stopped throwing up I gained weight very quickly. . Now I was going to have to break it to Jessie and my parents. Why can't things get easier for me I thought? At least I had stopped crying myself to sleep but I had started to sleep in Frank's bed on occasion. I thought that was my only way to be close to him. I still loved him so desperately and I was expecting two more reasons why.

I had lied to everyone, including Jessie about Frank's sudden departure. When I phoned Jessie I was at a loss to know what to say to him. The phone didn't even ring when he said. "How's the pregnancy mum, are you well?" I fell silent. "It's good." he said. "I was talking to Barry a week ago and he mentioned it to me. I was a little hurt that I had to hear it from him but it mustn't be easy for you. You know you have my full support, don't you?"

"You are the best mother anyone could have." he said. "Although I'm a little jealous, I know I will love he or she like a brother or sister." "Well," I said, "you might have one of each, I'm having twins." Now the phone went silent on his end.

"Wow, that's a handful." he said. "I've seen Barry and his wife with young James and they are exhausted half the time and there are two of them to take care of him. When are you due, are there any complications?" He just kept asking me questions. Now he sounded just like a doctor. "Well, it should be pretty easy to figure out," I said. "They tell me everything is quite normal and I have three more months to go." "Maybe I can take a break then," he said, "I'm still doing really well." "I'll let you know closer to the date." I said. "We can take it from there." "Now, I have to break the news to your grandparents." Jessie was so supportive and said he would keep in touch every day. Once a week would be fine, I told him.

Once I hung up the phone from Jessie, I had to phone my parents. They had never been judgemental, not even with my sister Alice who messed up constantly, although I was supposed to be the stable one. Now I had to break the news. "Twins." my Mother said. "How wonderful." I think I heard my Father groan. Fortunately, my mother insisted that she be here with me when the babies were born and she would stay as long as I needed her. I suggested 18 years, but she thought my father would think that excessive. I was so blessed to have understanding parents, family and friends rallying around to support me.

I looked like a blimp I thought to myself as I looked in the mirror. Only one more week to go. They should call it an eternity, not maternity, I thought to myself. The last few weeks had been hell. I didn't have any complications that I knew of but it was the excess weight in my belly. I tipped forward every time I stood up. I slowly sat down to have a late lunch. I hadn't been going into work for the last couple of weeks so I had had lots of rest. The water was boiling so I got up to get my tea. I no sooner stood up when my water broke, it was quick. I felt this big swoosh. It's too soon I said to myself as I picked up the

Tea, Love & Suspicion **147**

phone to call Mary at the office. She was my designated driver. She was at the door in 10 minutes. That was a record.

I was standing in the doorway waiting for her with my little suitcase in my hand. "I'm scared Mary, terrified more like it." "Everything is going to be just fine." she said, but I could hear her voice shaking. "I'll call your mother and Jessie once we get to the hospital, now relax, please, we'll be there in 5 more minutes, hold on." The twins were born at 2:00pm, twenty minutes after we arrived. Two identical boys gave their first breath. They were perfect.

CHAPTER FIFTY TWO

My mother arrived the next day. I was so glad to see her. It had been 21 years since I had even held a baby so I was going to have to practice. Somehow my mother took to it like a duck to water, what was wrong with me. Gail and Mary were a big help and even though Bert and Gail didn't have children they were wonderful. All four of them came home with me. Jessie arrived the next day so he missed the move in. He only had a couple of days before he had to get back so he spent all of his time with the boys. He will make a great father I thought as I watched him bathe and change them. The nursery was beautiful. I had cleared out Frank's bed and had the whole room newly decorated. Two cribs sat against the wall where their father's bed had been, it seemed appropriate. My mother stayed for a couple of weeks until my father ran out of food in the freezer but by that time, I was getting the hang of it.

Gail and Bert were constant visitors and suggested that if it was agreeable they would come over on a regular basis. Because of the money Margaret had left them, they had both retired and I think they were bored. They also suggested that if I wanted to go back to work they would love to baby sit for me, it was as if they had found a new lease on life, they were both wonderful. Along with Jessie's help we had decided to name the boys Frank and Harry. Harry was my father so he was pretty excited. Who knows what Frank's fathers' name was so it was up to me.

Tea, Love & Suspicion   149

The weeks passed quickly and before I knew it my boys were 9 months old. Even at that young age I talked to them about their father and how wonderful he was and how much I loved him. They may never see him but I wanted them to know how important he was. I started to work part time and occasionally I would take the boys into the office. Everybody went crazy when we came in and nothing got done for the next hour. I thought they were advanced for their age but everyone in the office remarked on how smart they were.

I read to them every night and played my favourite music for them. It was really strange. When I read to them they looked like they were listening to me and my music sent them to sleep. Jessie said no wonder. Your music sends everybody to sleep.

By the time they were a year old they were talking to each other and walking. I had heard of twins having their own language but they really did. I didn't understand a word of it so one night I said, "It's time boys, lets speak English so I can understand." They both turned to look at me and said, "Okay mummy." My jaw dropped and I just looked at them, no, I didn't hear right but from then on they spoke to me in words. Although, while they were in their room, they spoke their own language.

CHAPTER FIFTY THREE

The years passed so quickly and by their 6th birthday I had stopped thinking about Frank every day. I so wished he could have been there to see how intelligent the boys were and how they were head and shoulders above other children of their own age.

We always had a big birthday party for the boys and their 6th was no exception. All my office staff showed up, Gail and Bert of course and Mary and Fred who had stood by me through thick and thin and had become my very dear friends. Barry and his wife Patricia brought their son James over for the party. He was almost a year older but although the twins liked him, they seemed like they were much older. We had such a great time, the boys were the life of the party. When I had asked them what they wanted for their birthday, they said they wanted books and two Meccano sets each with the remote controls. I wondered what they would want for their 7th, a chemistry set. I couldn't believe how fast time passed. The boys were growing in leaps and bounds. They sure kept me busy. Between the boys and work there never was a dull moment.

It was almost 8 years since the night Frank had left and the years had been uneventful, other than the boys. I hadn't even been to the hotel for dinner in all that time. Too many memories. My body was in good shape, the boys were healthy and I had new found friendships. It was anything but boring and I

Tea, Love & Suspicion

loved Frank Jr. and Harry so much. When I thought they might never have been born, I felt sick.

CHAPTER FIFTY FOUR

I celebrated the 9th anniversary of Franks' departure, as I called it, with a trip to the hairdresser. I couldn't believe that it was only three months to another birthday. The years were going by so quickly. The boys had mastered their Meccano sets long ago and had built all sorts of mechanical devices. They built things not even shown on the pamphlets and they worked. Now I had to think of what to get them for their 8th birthday that was fast approaching. It wasn't going to be easy. I had never been able to surprise them once with gifts. I sat them down at dinner time and asked them what they would like this year. They looked at each other and said, "Daddy." Oh boy, I thought, that would be a miracle.

The day of the party came and all of the same people showed up to celebrate. They had all brought something for the boys and they were all lying on the kitchen table. Mary and Gail saw me looking at the gifts. Mary asked me what I had got for the boys, I said, "nothing, yet." "All they keep talking about is their father, that's all we want, they said. How can I do that Mary, I just wish I could."

Just then the doorbell rang. When I opened the door the man said he had a special delivery for Mrs. Bremner. "Yes," I said. "Please sign here ma'am." he said. It was just a plain envelope with my name on the front. "No return address?" I asked. "No Ma'am." he said.

Tea, Love & Suspicion 153

As I walked into the living room the twins said, "Told you so." I'm not sure what they meant but I was pre-occupied trying to open the envelope. Inside was a torn piece of paper, on it were the words, "I'll always love you, and don't forget it". I had to sit down, it was exactly the same as the note Frank had left me the night he disappeared.

I got up and ran up to my room and grabbed the paper that I had saved for all these years. The note that was delivered was a small piece that had been torn off my note and the tares matched perfectly. I started to cry. I knew it had to be from Frank, who else could it be? Or was this somebody's sick joke?

The boys came into my room and hugged me. "It's alright mum, daddy's coming home, isn't he?" I knelt down beside them and hugged them both. "I want that so badly," I said, "for all of us." The doorbell rang again. Damn, leave me alone I said to myself but maybe the delivery man had found the return address and I could find out where Frank was. I slowly made my way through the crowd still wiping away my tears. I opened the door. "Frank!" I let out a scream. He looked a little worse for wear but was just as beautiful as I remembered him to be. I could feel my knees buckling. He took me in his arms and kissed me like he had never been away. Frank Jr. and Harry were standing right behind me. As Frank knelt down the boys rushed into his arms. "We knew you were coming daddy." Everyone in the room was in tears, even the men. It was a birthday party to remember. I'd never be able to top this one I thought.

CHAPTER FIFTY FIVE

It had been 9 years since I had seen Frank. I know that there are many service men that had been missing even longer, but this was my man. I think it was just as well we had so many people around so I couldn't fall apart. It seems like forever before I could get everyone to leave the party. Poor Frank, he walked into a hornets nest. Everyone wanted to welcome him home. I think he hugged everyone and the tears of joy flowed throughout the house. Every couple of minutes he would bend down and hug the boys, they seemed to be the only ones that held it together. It was after 7 o'clock before everyone left and Frank and I got to hold each other.

When Frank picked up the boys, they were mirror images of their father. It seemed impossible. Frank wanted to put the boys to bed and I must admit I gave in quickly, I was exhausted. I listened at the door to hear what they were saying and to my surprise they were all talking that gibberish. How on earth could Frank understand what they were saying never mind the fact that he was talking back to them, I had to ask him when things settled down.

When he first came into the bedroom, he walked slowly towards me. "How did you do it Angela? I am so sorry I wasn't here for you but it's a long long story. The boys are perfect, they may look like me but they have your inner beauty." We sat on

Tea, Love & Suspicion 155

the bed and just held each other. It felt like a perfect ending to a perfect day.

"I'm exhausted my love and I know you have a million questions for me and I promise, I will answer all of them. But, first of all I have to ask you something." I made myself comfortable on the bed and waited, it seemed like he was being quite serious. He knelt by the bed and held my hand and said. "Angela Bremner, I would be honoured if you would marry me, not for the boys but because I wouldn't be alive today if it hadn't been for the love I have for you."

I sat straight up in bed and the tears flowed down my cheeks. "Oh yes." I said. As I fell into his arms. "I've been waiting all these years for you to come back to me and I never want you to leave me again." We kissed, gently, but somehow it had more feeling in it that one moment than I could have possibly imagined. "Mrs. Angela Winston, it sounds perfect." I said. "Well," he said, "not so fast. I'm afraid that's not exactly my real name."

At that moment there was a knock on the door. "Come in boys," I said. They came running in and jumped into Frank's arms. "We are so glad your back daddy. We sent messages to you just about every day." "I know." Frank said. I just couldn't believe the instant bond these three beings had for each other, it was like watching a science fiction movie. Sometimes you just have to accept things as they are, I thought, I would ask questions later. Frank took the boys back to bed

CHAPTER FIFTY SIX

When he came back into the room he was taking off his shirt. I just about screamed. "Oh, Frank, what did they do to you?" I cried. His chest and back were so badly scarred there was hardly a square inch that wasn't damaged. I jumped out of bed and gently stroked his body. The welts ran into each other. "It doesn't hurt," he said. I imagined the holes were bullet holes and it made me shudder. "Come to bed Frank you need to rest. You can tell me all about it tomorrow." I said. We held each other through the night and once in a while I heard him moaning in his sleep. I would find out some answers tomorrow so I drifted off into a perfect sleep with his arms around me.

I was woken up with a knock on the door. "Come in," I said, but be quiet, daddy's still sleeping. Let's let him to sleep a little longer, we can go have breakfast before you go to school maybe by that time he'll be awake and he can take you to school, if he feels up to it." "He's going to be fine mommy, really." the boys said. "I know he will," I said, "he's home." The boys gobbled down their breakfast and kept looking at the bedroom door. They started speaking gibberish to each other again. "Okay you two, I said, "I think I know what you're up to." Two minutes later Frank came out of the bedroom. "You woke him up didn't you?" I said.

"What would you like for breakfast Frank?" "Just toast and coffee would be great and then I can take the boys to school,

Tea, Love & Suspicion   **157**

if that's okay." "Perfect," I said. Both Frank Jr. and Harry were noticeably excited. I had put them in a special school for gifted children and they were responding well, even though I didn't think they were challenged as much as they should be. This wasn't exactly the best education they needed but until we found another outlet for them it would have to do. Now that Frank was home, we could discuss it. I gave Frank the keys to my car. His car was being taken away today, thank goodness. I was tired of listening to it talk to itself. It was so bad over the years that I even started answering it. As they headed out the door the boys gave me a hug and told me they loved me. Frank kissed me. "I won't be long." he said.

When Frank came back I was sitting at the kitchen table drinking my third cup of tea. I had so many questions running around in my head I was going crazy. He could see my agitation and came to me with open arms and I just folded into his body.

CHAPTER FIFTY SEVEN

Okay, Angela, I know you want to know everything but let me take it piece by piece. "My name isn't Frank Winston and I don't have a sister. I had a feeling that you thought I might have ran away with her. I didn't. Tara was to pass on some important information for my assignment, that's the only reason she was here. My real name is Michael Kingsford, but you can call me Frank." he smiled and so did I. "How does Angela Kingsford sound to you?" "Wonderful," I said. "When would you like to make this official?" "As soon as possible." he answered. "I want us to be a real family."

"Do you want a big wedding?" he said. "No definitely not." I answered. "In fact, I wouldn't mind a Las Vegas wedding, they are legal you know, and almost instant." Frank looked into my eyes and said. "I want you to do whatever you want, I want you to be happy and I'll be right beside you, forever." "Let me think," I said, "I just got over organizing a birthday party. Maybe we could go into the city and have a court house marriage. Do you have all your papers to do that?" "Well, I've never been married before so I'm not sure." At least that was a relief, I thought.

Frank said we could always have a military wedding. "Too many choices," I said, "I need to think." He picked me up and kissed me. "I love you so much Angela." "You are all I want Frank, Michael," I stuttered. "I don't think I'll ever get used to the name Michael." He was the love of my life and he was worth the years of wait. What's in a name any way.

CHAPTER FIFTY EIGHT

As the days passed I found out more about his life and I wondered how on earth he had survived. He had only been in Afghanistan for a year when he was captured and almost beaten to death. They held him for over four years trying to get information out of him. Apparently they had beaten him regularly. I gather the information he had was so important that the seals raided the place where they were holding him. His prison guards weren't giving him up easily, the seals had tried before. His captors obviously decided that if they couldn't get the information he had, nobody could, so they shot him.

The seals managed to get him out of the compound but he had been seriously wounded and was in a coma for months. They didn't think he would survive in fact his heart stopped twice as they tried to remove the bullets. Apparently Michael (Frank) was the only one who could unlock vital information they had so they had the best surgeons' possible working on him.

When he eventually came out of his coma he was having a conversation in a different language and they thought his mind had been damaged irreparably. They had even called in special linguists to try to understand what he was saying. I think somehow the boys could have translated. It took a year to bring him back and nine months of rehabilitation. He must be really important, I thought. He stayed there until they translated the

Tea, Love & Suspicion   **161**

information he had and then he was free to go back to his life. It had apparently taken another 6 months to get his head together. He had more than served his term.

I didn't know it but after he had left me, he had made arrangements to have me followed and watched over for as long as he was away. They were to report to him on my condition, when they could. All of my bills had been paid while he was away. I never could find out by whom. Now things were starting to add up.

Apparently he knew I was pregnant just about as soon as I did but he couldn't under any circumstances contact me. Not for his safety but for mine. He didn't find out about the twins until he came out of his coma. He said that without that information and the feeling he had for me, he might have given up.

We were married in a small ceremony 2 weeks after he came back and all our friends were there to support us. We didn't change Frank Jr. name. It was a beautiful reminder of how he came to be. Harry and Frank Jr. were a joy to have and I was totally content. I called our boys the friendly aliens, just like their dad.

When Dr. Jessie Bremner came home he spent all of his time with his not so little brothers. He loved the boys and the boys loved him. Jessie had met this wonderful girl and was planning to move to South America for a few years to do research. I was so happy for him. It was what he always wanted and Susan seemed like the perfect partner. She had as many degrees as Jessie had. It seemed like the perfect partnership. They were both looking forward to the challenges they were going to face, together. I could relax in the fact that I had faith they would be happy.

My business was thriving and all was well with the world. I still got kissed every morning and every night and many times in between and I kissed him right back. Who cares about the secrets that I know Frank still held. How was it that his scars were disappearing? What was the language he spoke with the boys? Who cares, I thought, he's mine.

CHAPTER FIFTY NINE

Frank had been home now for almost a year. I had the happy little family that I had dreamed of. We had discussed when Frank first came home that Frank was going to home school the boys until they were ready for University. It was really a good idea, Frank was incredibly intelligent and the boys loved having their father with them all day. I had my business to run so I was gone most days although I had started taking more time off. Mary was perfect, she took over the office when I was away and we were still making lots of money. It seemed like everyone was happy. Well, not quite.

Frank was so close to the boys that they didn't ask me for anything and I was feeling a little left out. Even when I stayed home for the day I hardly saw them, they just stayed in their room with Frank and studied. I guess. They came out for lunch and dinner and that was about it. I really hadn't been in their room for so long. "I don't want you to worry about the boys' room," Frank had said. "It's their responsibility and really, their doing a great job." So, I really hadn't been in their room for months. I had tried to take a look but the door was locked and I just left well enough alone. Frank would make sure it was clean. He was even neater than I was.

One night when we went to bed, Frank and I had had a discussion about sports. I thought the boys should get involved with some kind of activity, outside of the house. Living on the West coast gave us every opportunity for the boys to get involved in all kinds of things. The winter was almost over but the ski season was still in full swing on our local mountains. The ski hill was only half an hour drive from our home. In summer they could play tennis or whatever. I really thought it would be good for them and to my surprise, Frank agreed. "We'll take a day off studying tomorrow and I'll take the boys up to the ski hill and see what they think." "That sounds great." I said. "What time are we leaving?" "Well," Frank said slowly. "I thought for the first time maybe *I* should take them. They know what a good skier you are and they wouldn't like for you to see them falling all over the place. I'm sure they'll catch on pretty quick. Then we can all go together." I sat up in bed and looked at Frank in disbelief. "You are kidding, aren't you?" I said. "They really are *our* boys you know. *I* would like to spend some quality time with them as well." "*Please,* he said, "just this once. I really don't want you to see *me* falling. I want to get the hang of it first before we show you how good we are." Frank was impossible to say no to. He took me in his arms and kissed me. I melted.

CHAPTER SIXTY

I woke up early and although I was still miffed about not going skiing, I kind of understood. Frank was already making coffee in the kitchen. "What time are you leaving?" I said. "Well, I was thinking. We'll have to go into town first to get some warm clothes. The boys have grown out of their last winter jackets and it is time they got some new ones anyway". "So, if we leave around ten o'clock we should be home around two o'clock. How does that sound?" The boys came running into the kitchen. "Morning Mum." "What kind of sustenance do you have for these young explorers?" Harry said. "I need a hug before I feed anyone." I said. All three of them gathered around and hugged me. The boys were not even 8 years old yet and already they were almost as tall as me. "I'm being squished." I said as I came up for air. You know we love you, don't you mum." Frank Jr. said. "I know, I just miss the little boys I had. You are both growing so fast." I had to turn away. I could feel my eyes well up. "You are a big softy Mum." Harry said. "And, that's why we love you." How about scrambled eggs, sausage and toast *and where's my tea?" I shouted. "Doesn't anyone care about me anymore?"* All three of them ran to put the kettle on.

Frank gave me a kiss and a hug and thanked me for understanding. I watched as they loaded themselves into the Escalade, it was the perfect vehicle for the winter. Harry came running back in. "I forgot something." He said as he rushed by me. It was almost 10 o'clock by the time they left. The stores didn't open until ten anyway so there was no rush. At least they were out of the house. I thought it would be good for them. Now all I had to do was figure out what I was going to do for the day. I know what, I'll make some pasta, I said to myself. I had just bought one of those fancy machines that make pasta and I hadn't even opened the box yet. That would be my challenge for the day.

It wasn't as easy as it looks. I had flour all over the kitchen to say nothing of myself. Maybe I should have added more liquid, it seemed a little dry. Oh well, I had followed the instructions to the letter so it should work. I put the dough into the contraption and hoped it would figure it out. It seemed to work pretty well, not exactly as shown on the pamphlet but for a first attempt, I was pretty proud of myself. I covered it in Saran wrap and put it in the fridge. Once I had cleaned up the kitchen, I decided to vacuum the whole house. I started in our bedroom. Dust bunnies had definitely moved in behind the furniture. I always thought I did a good job of cleaning but, I thought of that old expression. *"If Man was made of dust, I would have created an army."*

It was only 12:30 so I thought I might as well do the rest of the house and then I would stop for lunch. I vacuumed the hallway and as I was vacuuming close to the boy's room the door opened. They must have forgotten to lock it. I couldn't help it, I had to look. I slowly opened the door.

CHAPTER SIXTY ONE

The room was so dark, where was the window? I turned on the light. The whole room was wall to wall chalk boards. Every one of them was covered in hieroglyphics. The boy's beds were pushed together in the middle of the room. I stood there with my mouth open. Surely the boy's didn't understand all of this. What were they learning? I went into the kitchen to get my cell phone. I wanted to take pictures so I could find out what it was. I had no sooner taken a couple of pictures when I heard the boys come home. They were early. It was no use trying to hide; I was caught in the act. I shoved my cell phone into my pocket.

Frank came into the room. "Where are the boys?" I asked. "I just sent them for a walk to the park." he said as he slowly walked into the room. "I bet your wondering what we have done with the room, aren't you?" he said. I could hardly speak my mouth was so dry. I just looked at him. "Who are you?" I said. "I'm the man that loves you. Come here Angela; sit on the bed with me. I need to talk to you." The door to the bedroom was still open and I thought about making a run for it. Although Frank hadn't said anything to scare me, I knew he was upset, he was talking slower than usual. I decided to sit on the bed. "You know I love you, don't you Angela?" "You are my reason for living. You are my reason for being here." "I know I said, but I miss my babies, my boys and I feel like I'm not needed." It was different when the boys were young." Frank hadn't really changed towards me.

He was still loving and caring. He still kissed me and held me morning noon and night. I must have looked pretty sad as tears drifted down my cheeks. He held me in his arms. "My poor Angela, I'm so sorry to upset you but it's a little complicated and top secret. Some of what you see on the chalk boards are things I am working on for the Government and the others are what I am working on with the boys." He reached into my pocket and took out my cell phone. "If pictures got out showing some of the work I've been doing, I will be in real trouble. Do you mind if I erase them?" I looked at the phone and then at him. "Sure, go ahead" I said. "How did you know?" Now I was thinking, how the heck did he know I had taken pictures? He hadn't come into the room until after I had put it in my pocket. As if he knew what I was thinking he held my hand. "Because I would have done exactly what you did, so how can I blame you?" He held me tight and kissed me. I instantly became incredibly aroused. He lay me down and started making love to me. I don't know why but I couldn't stop, in-fact, I became so passionate I became the aggressor. Just like the first time we made love. "What about the boys?" I moaned. "Don't worry they won't come back till I tell them." I heard what he said but I was too far gone to really comprehend. All I wanted was him. Although we had made love many times since he came back into my life, there was nothing to compare with the first time, until now. It was as if my whole body was part of his and I couldn't get enough. My whole body undulated trying to get him deeper inside me.

I wasn't sure how long we had made love but I needed to catch my breath. "Let's go to our room." he said as he picked me up off the bed. He wrapped a sheet around us and carried me into our bedroom. Just as I closed the door behind us, as if on cue, I heard the boys come in through the front door. How about that for incredible timing I thought. Frank and I continued our love making in the shower. I was exhausted. He dried me off and gently placed me on the bed. He lay beside me resting on one elbow. He looked into my eyes. "You are the most perfect woman Angela. When your husband passed away, you took charge. Even when you were in that terrible storm so many years ago, you just kept going. You never gave up. That's part of what makes you so special. Your kind, smart and thoughtful to mention only a few of the reasons I love you." Something he had said bothered me but I couldn't put my finger on it. I was so exhausted I really didn't care. He lay beside me and just held me for the longest time. I was lost in his arms. He kissed me gently and walked to the door. "Relax Angela," he said. That was the last thing I remember. I drifted off into a beautiful sleep. When I woke up I thought I could smell something cooking so I got dressed and walked into the kitchen.

They were boiling water for my pasta. "I hope it turns out okay boys, I said, I've never made it before so you're taking a big chance." "I thought I would put some of that tomato sauce you make on it, what do you think?" Frank said. "Anything sounds good to me right now, I'm starving." I said as I set the table. The boys came over to me and hugged me. "We really didn't like skiing mum, do we have to do it?" Harry said. "No Harry, but I would really like to see you both get involved in some kind of outside activity. It can be anything you want. Sometimes when you try something and get good at it, you begin to love it. One time is hardly a fair trial." "But it's freezing up there and all those people." Frank Jr. said. "Yes, I said, people. I know you have each other but you don't really have any other friends." "Your right Angela, we really should find something for the boys to do, right boys?" Frank said. "Okay, the boys said in unison, we'll try. But not skiing." We all laughed. I loved skiing but it wasn't for everyone. "Maybe in the summer we can go sailing, I think you would like that." I said. The boys looked at each other. "That sounds good." They said. With that, we sat down to eat dinner. The pasta was pretty good, especially for a first attempt. I'm sure most people would have thought I was crazy for not questioning Frank but it was as if I was lost in his charm and the love I had for him and the boys. I was still independent but I knew one day my doubts would come to a head and I would challenge him. For now, I would wait till the time was right for me.

CHAPTER SIXTY TWO

After the boys went to bed Frank and I watched TV. Frank sat to face me. "I want to take you out to dinner tomorrow night would you like to go to the hotel?" "I love it there, I said, it's been so long since we have been out for dinner, it will be a real treat, I think the boys would like it too." "No, Frank said, just the two of us." "We can get Bert & Gail to look after the boys, although I think the boys actually look after them rather than the other way around." "I'll phone them now and see if they can." I said. Gail answered on the first ring. I think she said yes before I even asked the question. They were so happy that I had called. They loved the boys and were glad to come over. Take all the time you want they said, we haven't seen the boys for weeks. As I hung up the phone, Frank kissed me. "How about a date Mrs. Kingsford?" "Well, I'll have to ask my husband." I said. Frank picked me up spun me around and kissed me. "I'm really looking forward to a night out with you, it's been too long." "Yes my love, your right." I said as I kissed him back. It seemed like the old Frank was back, the Frank I loved so desperately. "How about I light the fire?" He said. I looked at him and smiled, "You know where the wood is."

The boys did their regular studying through the day although they had left the door open a couple of times. I suppose it was to let me know they had no secrets, even though I suspected they did. I decided to wash my hair and put an oil pack on.

My hair had become really dry so I had bought two packs just the other day. It had been a long time since I pampered myself. I climbed into the shower and washed my hair. I towel dried it and put the oil on and pulled it down to my split ends and combed it through. I didn't want to put a towel on without something in between so I went to the kitchen and put saran wrap around my head and then covered it with aluminum foil, then I put the towel on. I was bound and determined to get to those split ends. I thought the warmth of the wrapping would help the treatment.

I had no sooner put the towel on my head when I could hear Frank shouting for me." Angela, Angela!" I walked out of the kitchen and there was Frank. "What's wrong Frank?" "Is there a problem?" He looked so perplexed "No, I'm okay. I just wondered where you had got to, what's that on your head?" "I just put an oil treatment on my hair." I said. "What is it?" he asked. I showed him the product and he read the whole package. "Somehow I really don't think this stuff is very good for you." he said. "It smells strange. Maybe you should wash it off." "I just need another 15 minutes and then I'm done. I've used this before and it really helped." He looked at me and looked at my turban. "Okay, he said, 15 minutes." He just turned around and went back into the boys' bedroom. What the heck was that all about I wondered? He seemed really strange. He had a look on his face I had never seen before. He seemed bewildered. It was obvious that he was allergic to something. I guess he was vulnerable to some things after all. My 15 minutes were up and I climbed back into the shower and shampooed my hair, it felt great. I balled up the foil and saran wrap and threw it in the kitchen trash. I thought if Frank didn't like the smell or had an allergy, I would keep it out of our bedroom.

"What time did you ask Gail and Bert to come over?" Frank asked. I shouted to him from the bathroom. "They said

Tea, Love & Suspicion **173**

they would be here by 6:45 so you better start to get ready, it's already 6:15 and you haven't showered yet. "I was hoping we could conserve on water and shower together but I guess I'm a little late." He said as he came into the bathroom. "I know you and showers Michael Kingsford, you are on your own tonight." I never could get used to the name Michael but sometimes I would tease him. To me Frank suited him much better.

CHAPTER SIXTY THREE

Our reservations were for 7:30, we had lots of time. I just thought it would be nice to have a bit of a visit with Gail and Bert. We hadn't seen them for a while. I fed the boys the left over pasta, so they were fed and already in their pyjamas. I looked into my closet for something nice to wear and I came across my little black dress, perfect, I thought. I had just finished getting ready when the doorbell rang. It had to be Gail and Bert. Both Frank Jr. and Harry really liked them. They both rushed to answer the door. I heard this deep voice say. "I'm looking for a Mr. Michael Kingsford." "Somebody at the door for you Dad," the boys shouted. It was strange to hear someone calling him Michael, but it *was* his real name, everyone I knew, including me had always called him Frank.

As he walked to the door I could see that he was hesitating. I heard him say, "Oh, its you." and stepped outside. I gather that Gail and Bert interrupted their conversation as they came to the door. "Go ahead, Frank said, I'll be in in a minute." He closed the door behind him. The boys came and gave them a big hug. "We missed you." Harry said. And we missed both of you terribly Gail said as she gave them both a kiss on the head. All of a sudden I realized that when it came time to put the boys to bed, they would be going into the boy's bedroom. "I'll be back in a minute, just make yourself comfortable." I said. As I walked the landing to the boy's room I wondered if Frank had thought of this problem. I opened up the door and it was as if the chalk boards had never existed. The boys beds were against the wall, the window was visible and the furniture was back in place. I looked into the walk in closet and there were the chalk boards, stacked in the corner. I should have known better, of course he thought of it.

We had a nice visit with Bert and Gail. The strange man with the deep voice had left and we were on our way to the Hotel. "It's been a long time." Tom said as he greeted us at the hotel. "You are looking as beautiful as ever Mrs. Kingsford." "Thank you Tom, I'm feeling pretty good tonight." "How are the boys doing?" He said. "I haven't seen them for a while?" "There doing great, growing like weeds." I replied. I think that was the second longest conversation I had ever had with Tom at the hotel. When we met in the village we would chat for ages and catch up on how our old school mates were doing, but when he was at work, he was the consummate professional.

When we walked into the restaurant we notice that our favourite table had "Reserved" on it so we didn't go to it straight away like we used to. Nancy the hostess greeted us and showed us to our table and took the reserved sign with her. Somehow, it was important that we have this table tonight, it had wonderful memories. I could see that Frank was hoping for it too. As the evening advance I mentioned to Frank that it was a good thing he moved his chalk boards otherwise we would have heard it all over town. "I know." said Frank. "I was amazed we got it together so fast, the boys did most of the work." "It was nice of you to check it out though. And, by the way, your hair looks beautiful. Too bad that stuff smells so bad." "Well, I only do it once in a while so I'll pick a time when you are out next time." I said. It was like old times, we chatted away, it was nice that we hadn't lost that interest in each other. We used to watch couples sitting eating and they never said a word to each other.

They must be married, we would say. "Who was that man at the door tonight Frank? He sounded pretty official." "He's with a Government agency and was wondering if I had finished my project." he said. "Why didn't he just phone you, I would think that would be faster." I said. "Well, telecommunication is not exactly the safest way to communicate. In fact, if you have anything of a sensitive nature it's probably the worst way to communicate." "I guess your right about that, Big Brother is watching, isn't he?" I said as Frank ran his credit card through the hotel POS. All too soon it was time to go home. The meal had been fantastic. The Prime Rib was cooked to perfection and the vegetables where perfectly steamed.

CHAPTER SIXTY FOUR

As I got up to leave the table, I felt dizzy. Frank caught me just before I fell and sat me back down. "Are you Okay Angela, what's wrong?" Frank said as he knelt beside me. "I don't know, I said, I just felt really weird. I feel fine now, let me stand up." As I got up from the chair, the moment had passed. It was just a fleeting feeling. Then it was gone.

As we left the restaurant I felt normal again although Frank wouldn't let go of my arm. "Are you sure you're okay Angela you had me worried." I had only felt this way once before and that was when I was pregnant. It couldn't be that this time because when the boys were born, I had a tubal ligation. It was probably from sitting so long on a very full stomach. If it happened again, I would get it checked out.

When we got home Frank was very attentive. I think I scared him when I almost fainted at the restaurant. He held my hand in the car and he never took his hand off my arm until we got into the house. "I'm fine, really, I said to him, it was just a momentary thing and it passed." As we walked thought the door Bert and Gail were there to greet us. "How about a cup of tea Gail, come into the kitchen and we can chat." We left Bert and Frank in the living room. "Tell me Gail, how have you been keeping, are you planning any holidays?" "No, she said, although we were looking into a cruise in May, it sounded like fun although Bert will need a little encouragement." "How were the boy's tonight?" I asked, "Did they give you any trouble?" I asked even though I knew the answer would be no. "You know Angela, those boys are so smart and they have grown like weeds. Harry was such a chatter box tonight. He was telling me how he hated skiing but he thought he might like going out sailing this summer, he actually sounded quite enthusiastic, even young Frank was going on about it. Are you planning on taking up sailing again?" "Well, it's a thought." I said. "I would love to get them interested in something other than studies. They are like little sponges and Frank is doing a wonderful job teaching them but they do need to socialize." "Yes, I think your right." Gail said "But you are really lucky. They are such sweet boys." We finished our tea and joined the men in the living room. "Well Gail, it's about that time". Bert said. It was only 10 o'clock but I guess they went to bed early these days. We hugged them and thanked them and they told us to call them anytime.

When I was getting ready to go to bed Frank came up behind me and put his arms around me. His hands caressed my breast and then my belly. He snuggled his head in my neck and kissed me on the ear. "You are my super woman Angela and I'll always be here to take care of you." I turned to face him. I put my hands on his face and pulled him towards me and kissed him. "I know." I said.

CHAPTER SIXTY FIVE

I had planned to go to the office the next day so I was up early. It seemed like everyone hit the kitchen door at the same time. "I'm just having tea this morning so Frank, you're up for the boys breakfast." "No problem." he said as he made his coffee. He had become a pretty good cook and I wanted to get into the office before anyone else for a change. I had taken too many days off in the last couple of weeks and I was hoping we might have some news on a contract we had bid for.

It actually felt good to go to the office, I felt like I was accomplishing something. I loved my home life but I also needed to keep my brain working and if we got this new contract my whole office would be crazy busy. I put the coffee pot on, plugged the kettle in and went into my office. Mary had kept me posted as to what was going on so I knew there would be no surprises in my in basket. Just as I was sifting through the papers, Mary came into my office with her coffee and my tea. "I've missed you." She said. "Nobody talks to me in the morning like you do." she said as she plunked herself down on my sofa. "How are the boys and Frank doing? I haven't seen them for a while." "Good", I said, Frank is taking them into the city next week for a meeting with the Dean of Watson College. Frank just wants to see how their studies are progressing and if they are in line with the College. They haven't turned eight yet but they are so advanced for their age we don't want them to get bored with their studies. "Good grief." Mary said. "You have a couple of geniuses on your hands. I'll have to come over for a visit before they leave for University." "Don't laugh." I said. "That could be any day now." We both laughed and finished our drinks.

By the time I sifted through my paperwork it was 11:30. "I'm going to grab and early lunch Mary, I'll just be in the Cafe across the street if you need me. Maybe if I leave we'll hear something on that contract." Mary gave me the thumbs up and I gave her the victory sign. That ritual always seemed to bring us luck in the past so hopefully it would work today.

I was starving. No breakfast was not a good idea. I ordered a BLET (bacon, lettuce, egg and tomato) with fries and a milk shake. I had just started into my lunch when Mary came into the cafe with a man. "Sorry Angela, this is Mr. Dixon regarding the contract we were waiting for." "I am so sorry to interrupt your lunch Mrs. Kingsford but I had to change to an earlier flight and I'm afraid I'll have to cut my visit with you shorter than I had planned. In fact, if you don't mind I would really like to join you for a quick lunch." "My pleasure." I said, "The food here is really quite good." The hair on the back of my neck was doing a tap dance. As Mary left she looked at me and gave me that shaking of the hand to let me know she thought he was, as she called it, hot. And he most definitely was. He was extremely attractive. In fact as we sat chatting and eating our lunch, I was amazed that I was enjoying his company so much. I was actually sorry he had to leave so quickly but we had agreed that our contract was a fair one and he presented me with the signed agreement. He shook my hand, "By the way, he said, my name is Simon." "And mine is Angela." He told me he would be in touch again very soon and left. He had no sooner turned the corner when Frank walked into the cafe. "Well, this is a surprise," I said, "what brings you into this neighbourhood?"

Tea, Love & Suspicion 181

He was looking around the cafe, as if he was searching for someone. "No reason, he said, I just thought I would stop by and say hello." He sat down at the table and was looking at the dishes. Why did I feel guilty, I hadn't done anything but I got the feeling that Frank was thinking otherwise.

"Well Frank, I have to get back to work. We've just landed this wonderful contract and I can't wait to give them the good news in the office. Why don't you come with me?" I said. "No. It's okay, he said, I should get back to the boys anyway." With that he kissed me and was on his way. When I walked into the office, I tried to look as if I was upset but I couldn't keep it up. The office staff was lined up waiting. "We got it!" I yelled. "Coffee all round." Everybody cheered. This contact was well within our expertise and was really lucrative. We were all really excited. "How about dinner at the hotel tomorrow night?" I said. "Let me know and I'll make reservations." All I heard was yes, yes, yes that was 14 yeses. "Good enough Mary, come see me in my office." I phoned and made reservations. Just as I hung up the phone Mary came in. "Oh, my God Angela, that Mr. Dixon is about the hottest man I have ever seen. Except for Frank of course." "I know what you mean, I said, he's almost too good looking." "Simon had no sooner left the cafe, when Frank walked in." Mary looked at me. "It's Simon, is it Angela? He told me his name was Mr. Dixon." We both laughed. "What was Frank doing in town?" Mary asked. "I don't know," I said slowly, "it was as if he was looking for someone and when he saw that there had been someone else sitting at the table with me I think he was jealous. How could that possibly be? He didn't come into the cafe until after Simon had left." "You got me, Mary said, I think maybe Frank is a bit psychic, actually a lot psychic." She was right. There were so many co-incidences. I had to think this one through. "Mary, I said, "did you tell Frank where I was?" She shook her head.

CHAPTER SIXTY SIX

On my way home that night after work, I stopped at the Bakery and picked up a fresh apple pie. I had been thinking about apple pie ever since lunch. I couldn't wait to get home and cut a nice big slice. I kept wondering if I still had some vanilla ice cream left or if I should pick some up. I couldn't take a chance; I stopped at the grocery store. I couldn't believe it, I was actually salivating just thinking about this stupid apple pie. When I walked through the door the boys were there to greet me. "Hello mum, Harry said, did you have a good day?" "Perfect." I said. "Although I am going to be pretty busy for the next couple of weeks, how was your day?" Frank Jr. seemed really excited and came running toward me. "Dad has set up our test for next week and I'm really looking forward to it, dad said we should have no problems, only trouble is, it's a two day session in the city and I really don't like cities." "Well, I said, at least you don't have to live there. It'll be fun to stay in a hotel." "Yuk" was all I heard.

"Sorry boys, I have to have a slice of apple pie, how about you two." I said as I headed for the kitchen. "Where's your father?" Harry was right behind me. "He's in the shower." "He better hurry up otherwise there won't be any pie left." Frank came up behind me and kissed me on the top of my head. "You better leave me a piece." he said. "It's my favourite too." I have never seen a whole pie disappear so quickly. "I know it's not really

Tea, Love & Suspicion   **183**

good to have desert before dinner but I couldn't help myself." I said as I cleared our plates off the table. "I don't think any of us minded, did we boys," Frank said. "You should have got two."

Frank had already cooked dinner and it was in the warming oven so there was no rush. We all sat at the kitchen table and I found out Frank had been gone just about all afternoon. I wasn't too concerned that the boys had been on their own. They were smarter than most 30 year olds and they were really responsible but I wanted to know where Frank had been.

"Where did you go after I saw you this afternoon?" I asked. "I know I'm taller than you but didn't you notice my new hair cut?" Frank said. "OOps," I said as I looked at the boys. "You mean a head shave, don't you?" "Then where did you go?" I asked. "Well, I went to the car dealership to look at a new vehicle, and guess what?" "You're kidding, I said, you didn't buy a new car did you?" "No, I just looked." he said as he smiled and walked away. Our Escalade wasn't even a year old and my Lexus was even newer, not that it mattered, he could buy whatever he wanted. He had lots of money and we had minimal expenses. Neither of us had extravagant taste. Until it came to vehicles. I had envisioned a Ferrari parked in our garage and why not if he wanted one.

Once we had dinner and put the boys to bed, it was time to talk. "How is it that you know so much about what I'm thinking Frank, I'm getting to the point that I think you're in my head." He looked shocked. I had never challenged him or asked him direct questions about anything. "I guess I just love you to the point that supersedes reason. I used to do that with my Aunt and it drove her crazy but when she got sick I knew long before anyone else. She thought she had kept it a secret but I knew. In answer to your question, I really don't know." "I didn't even know you had an Aunt," I said. "Well, she's been gone for many years, most of my family died very young, in fact, I'm the only one left. How sad is that." I said. I gathered that Tara didn't count, or did she.

"While we are on the subject of family, I would really like to take the boys to see my parents. I was talking to them the other day and my father would like to introduce you and the boys to fishing and if Jessie can get away, he'll come too. It wouldn't be until May but I told them we would. They are not getting any younger and I really do miss them." "That sounds great, Frank said, but now that the boys have grown so much I think your father will have to buy a bigger boat." "You know what Frank. I think if that's what it would take to get us there, he would." "Settled." Frank said, as he kissed me. "You pick the date and we'll go."

CHAPTER SIXTY SEVEN

Work kept me busy and some days we even had to work overtime. It was nice having Frank at home at this time so I didn't have to worry about the boys. It was coming up to the time when they would leave for the city. I think Harry was more excited than Frank Jr. Although they were identical, Harry had a much better sense of humour. Frank Jr. was much more serious but had that wonderful gentleness at the same time. I was hoping that they would enjoy their trip and not worry too much about the tests. After all, they weren't even 8 years old yet.

"What time are you leaving tomorrow?" I asked Frank. "Our first appointment is at 2 o'clock Thursday but we'll leave around 9 o'clock and take our time. The other appointment is on Friday at 3 o'clock. We should be home for dinner and probably really hungry for home cooking." "I got it, I said, I'll have a fantastic dinner waiting for you."

As I was leaving for work the next day Frank and the boys were getting ready for their trip. I kissed Frank and the boys. "I'll miss you Angela, do you want me to pick up anything for you in the city?" I was in a bit of a rush but I couldn't imagine what we might need that we didn't already have. "No, I can't think of anything at the moment. We really don't need anything but you could always pick out some new clothes for the boys. With so many stores to choose from, the boys would probably get a kick out of it." Frank walked me to the door. "Good idea, they're growing so fast they really don't have much to wear these days, I'll see what we can find."

I got to work just in time to see Mary walking in ahead of me. We headed for the kitchen. We had been spending a lot of time working on our new clients' project and it was working out really well.

"Did Frank and the boys leave for the city yet?" She asked. "I would think so, I said, they were pretty well packed by the time I left. Frank said he would probably take it easy on the way down. The boys haven't been to the city before so they will probably be impressed. It's a different world from here".

"I really hate the city." Mary said. "The traffic alone drives me crazy and I hate tall buildings. Last time I was there I had to go into a high rise to visit my aunt. She was on the 29th floor and I could have sworn I could feel the building sway, it made me ill." "I know what you mean, I feel the same way." I couldn't help but shudder at the thought of it myself. I hated heights.

"Have you heard from Mr. Dixon," Mary asked. "Oh, I almost forgot, he phoned just after you left last night, he's really pleased with what we have been doing and he may come for a visit in a couple of weeks. Apparently he has some other business to look after and would be driving through anyway." "I think he likes you Angela." Mary said as she shook her finger at me. "I must admit Mary, he really made me feel uncomfortable when I met him. The hairs on my neck were working overtime, but I feel totally different when I talk to him on the phone." Mary was making my tea again. "I can see what you mean but we certainly have been doing a good job, I think. It's been a lot easier than I thought it would be." Just then, the phone rang in my office.

CHAPTER SIXTY EIGHT

I ran to my office and picked up the phone. "Hello, I said, "Bremner Consulting, can I help you?" All I heard was my mother mumbling on the other end of the line. "Mum, what's wrong?" "It's your father, he's in hospital." "What happened?" I said. "He had a fall and broke his hip but he's not taking it too well and I'm really worried." She was in tears. I looked at Mary who was standing in the doorway. "I'll catch the first flight I can, so don't worry I'll be there later today, I'll let you know what time. What hospital is he in?" "The City Hospital." She managed to say between her tears. Mary had already given me the thumbs up I could see her going to the phone, she would make all the arrangements while I consoled my mother. They had never been away from each other as long as they had been married so she was understandably upset.

"I better let Frank know what's going on." I said to Mary. As I dialled his cell phone I was looking at the note Mary had handed to me with my flight information. Franks' phone just rang and rang. What the heck is wrong with his messaging system? At least it didn't say that the line had been disconnected but I had to try to get hold of him. I looked up the phone number of the Watson College and dialled the number. "My name is Angela Kingsford, could I please talk to the Dean." I asked. "One moment." the operator said. "Dean Phillips here, can I help you?" "My name is Angela Kingsford and I understand my husband, Frank Kingsford has an appointment with you this afternoon. I apologize for calling you but we have a medical emergency in the family and I would like to reach my husband. He's coming in with our two boys for a meeting this afternoon." I blurted out.

There was silence on the line for a moment. A pregnant pause, I think they call it. "I'm sorry Mrs. Kingsford, I really don't seem to find an appointment this afternoon, are you sure you have the right number? If you can wait just a moment I will check with my secretary just to make sure." "Thank you. I really appreciate your help." He put me on hold for what seemed to be an eternity. "I'm sorry Mrs. Kingsford, I have nothing this week or next booked in under that name." "I must have made a mistake, I said, but I thank you for your time."

As I hung up the phone I just stared into space. I knew for sure that this was the College that Frank had told me. He had mentioned it a few times. I had attended that same College taking my Business degree so I knew it well. Mary broke my stare. She had heard the conversation and looked as perplexed as I did. "Just go, see your father she said, I'll keep trying Franks' number till you land." I was still shaken but had to get moving. I hurried home, packed a few things and headed for the airport. I phoned Mary from the airport but she hadn't been able to connect with Frank and there still was no messaging service.

I tried Franks' phone just before I walked into the hospital. No response. He had my boys, where was he?

As I walked into my fathers' room, my mother was at his side. We hugged and she cried. "What's wrong with you two?" my father said, "I'm fine." He really didn't look fine, he seemed pale and older. "The doctor said I'm going to be as good as new, they put me in a new titanium hip and said I should be ready to go fishing by May, so there." My mother didn't look so sure but I had to keep a positive attitude. "How long can you stay

Tea, Love & Suspicion

Angela?" my mother asked. "For as long as you need me." I said, although my mind was drifting to my two boys, who were who knows where.

CHAPTER SIXTY NINE

I stayed until the nurse asked us to leave. I no sooner got outside and turned my phone on when it rang. It was Mary. "I'm sorry Angela, I just tried Franks' number again and there is still no answer, what else can I do?" "Nothing, I said, I'll keep trying myself and thank you Mary I don't know what I would do without you." "Any problems?" my mother asked. "No. Nothing. Just keeping in touch with the office." I said. If only she knew I was sick with worry both for my father and for my family. My mother had told me my father had possibly had a small heart attack that caused his fall so they were keeping him in hospital for a few days and I promised I would stay until he came home.

There had to be a logical reason for Franks' silence. He would be home tomorrow night for sure, I told myself. Maybe he lost his phone but then again, the Dean didn't have any knowledge of his appointments. I felt like I was going to throw up.

As soon as we got back to my parents' home, we almost ran to the kitchen to put the kettle on. At least I knew where I got my tea fetish from. It was really difficult for me to keep a positive attitude but it's amazing how when you have to, somehow you find the strength. Before going to bed I gave Frank one more call. No answer.

When I woke up in the morning I was totally disoriented and I was actually sick to my stomach. No wonder, I thought as I reached for my phone. Still no answer. As we sat down for breakfast I couldn't shake the feeling of nausea. "Are you alright Angela?" my mother asked. "I just feel a little off colour mum, just concerned, that's all." "When was the last time you had a check-up?" she asked. "I'm fine really, what time do you want to go to the hospital?" "Anytime." she said. "I would sleep there if they would let me." "I just want to have a fast shower and we can go. I'll be fast." Mum was ready hours ago. "Sounds good to me, she said, I'll warm up the car."

Just before we walked into the hospital Mary phoned. I hated turning off my phone but cell phones were supposed to be off in the hospital so I had no choice. "The office is doing just fine." Mary said. "I took it upon myself to check for accidents and actually phoned hospitals in the city, just in case they had a problem but the good news is, there has been nothing reported. Sorry Angela, I can't wait to get my hands on Frank for the worry he's caused." Well, I said, he's not supposed to be back till tonight so I guess he's not late, yet, but he better call me or I'll be first in line to beat him up. I have to turn my phone off now so I'll talk to you later and thanks again Mary, you're the best."

My father was still looking a little under the weather but he was still his cheerful self. I loved that man so much. He had been and still was, my strength. "I would like to talk to Dr. Willson, if you don't mind mum. I just wish Jessie was here, he would know all the right questions to ask." My mother looked at my father. "Dr. Willson said he would call in this morning to see how your father is doing, so I would imagine he should be here pretty soon." We all chatted for about an hour like there was nothing wrong but I could see that my father was in pain. When Dr. Willson came into the room, he reached for his chart before he even said hello. "I'll be back in a minute." He said as he walked out of the room. Almost immediately the nurse came in and gave my father his pain medicine.

"He seems to be doing really well, the doctor said, but I would like to keep him in here for a couple more days." "Whatever you think, doctor." my mother said as she held my father's hand. They looked so sweet together I thought.

CHAPTER SEVENTY

"Could I have a word with you Dr. Willson?" I said. "Of course, he said, just walk with me, I have to get a glass of water." As we walked down the corridor I could feel myself starting to faint and I grabbed hold of his arm to save myself. It was as it was before, just a momentary feeling like a wave. Dr. Willson held me up and looked straight into my eyes. "Are you pregnant Angela?" he asked. "Oh my God, I hope not," I said as I gripped his arm. "Come with me, he said. I have an hour before I have to leave, I just want to give you a simple test, then we'll both know." Under the present circumstance, I didn't know if I even wanted to know but being pregnant was impossible so why not confirm it. As we walked into an examination room, I was nervous but Dr. Willson had known me for years so I felt comfortable indulging him in his prognosis.

It really didn't take long at all. It was a small rural hospital so they had a little more latitude than the large hospitals had. I was sitting on the examination table when Dr. Willson came back into the room. "Well Angela, I have good news, you're not sick. But you are pregnant. I fainted for real this time. As I came too I was back on the bed looking into a rather serious face. "Sorry Doctor, I said, I had a tubal ligation after my twins were born 8 years ago so you can imagine, it's a shock." "Well, he said, you can always check with your local Doctor, but I've never been wrong yet." he said as he patted my leg. Now what the hell am I going to do now, I thought.

"Please, I asked, don't mention anything to my parents yet." "Of course he said, your results are yours and only yours." "I'm sorry Dr. Willson all I really wanted to ask you was how my father was doing. "Did he have a heart attack?" "No. He tripped on a curb and was knocked off balance. When his body hit the pavement he landed square on his hip. He shouldn't have any lingering problems so long as he takes it easy. His hip turned out perfectly, so no worries." "Would he still be able to do some fishing?" I asked. "Yes, so long as he doesn't over-do it. Lifting boats is out of the question of course." He obviously knew my father. We actually laughed.

My mind was now switched to Frank. Now what, I wondered. Surely Frank hadn't left me again. My mind was going in circles. My parents, Frank, my boys, pregnant. I was totally mixed up. One second I was dealing with one thing and the next second it was something else. I would have to deal with one thing at a time or I would go mad.

We had a good visit with my father and I could tell that my mother was feeling much better. I told them what the doctor had said about fishing. "Maybe I should get one of those blow up boats'" he said. "Not a bad idea." I said.

CHAPTER SEVENTY ONE

As we left the hospital I turned my phone on. There were two messages. I couldn't wait to see who it was. I didn't recognize either number. It was Frank. He had lost his phone and would be home around 6 o'clock. The second message was also from Frank. He had phoned the office and found out about my father's accident and asked me to call him at home so we could talk. I could hardly wait.

It was only 5 o'clock when we left the hospital so I had another agonizing hour to wait until I could reach Frank. I had decided not to ask him about his trip to the College, I would save that for when I could ask him face to face.

6 o'clock could not come soon enough as I paced back and forth in the kitchen. My mother kept watching me pacing until she couldn't stand it anymore. "Stay still Angela. I'm getting dizzy just watching you go back and forth, what's the matter?" "Nothing really. Frank took the boys to the city and when I tried to call him his phone messages weren't getting through to him and I was worried that he may have left me and taken the boys." I blurted it out without taking a breath. My mother looked at me in disbelief and ushered me to sit down while she put the kettle on. "Angela, do you not trust Frank?" "I don't know mum, I sometimes think he may just leave me like he did before, I guess I never really got over the fact that he just disappeared one day without warning. I really do love him but

I sometimes think I don't really know him." I took a breath and sat down.

"Frank is so close to the boys mum, I hardly get any time to spend with them anymore, it's so different from raising Jessie." We sat silent for a few minutes. Mum got up to make the tea. "Have you talked to him about this Angela?" she sat down beside me and put her arms around me. "You have to talk to him Angela. You had the boys to yourself for 7 years. Maybe he's just trying to make up for lost time." "Its funny mum, even when we didn't know whether Frank was alive or dead, the boys knew. They were literally waiting for him to come back. Even when he wasn't there, the boys would talk to him as if he was in the same room. It bothered me but at the same time, it was re-assuring." Just then the phone rang, it was 6 o'clock exactly.

CHAPTER SEVENTY TWO

"I'm so sorry Frank said, how's your father doing?" "As well as can be expected." I said. "He fell and broke his hip. The Dr. said he is recovering well but wants to keep him in the hospital for a couple more days." "I couldn't believe I lost my phone." Frank said. "It must have been when we stopped for lunch but when I called the restaurant they said nobody had turned one in, so I was stuck." I could sense his nervousness. "Are you staying at your parents' house till your father comes home?" He said. "Yes." I said. All of a sudden I felt drained. All the worry and the thoughts that I might be pregnant was catching up to me. "I'm glad your all back, safe and sound, I said, I should be back some time on Monday or Tuesday, I'll let you know." There was silence on the other end of the phone. "Are you alright Angela, you sound strange?" "I'm fine now, I said, just a lot to deal with here and I was worried about you and the boys. I'll give you a call at the house tomorrow morning?" "Sounds good." Frank said. "The boys are tired so I think we will all have an early night, you could probably use some rest too. Give my love to your mum and dad from me and the boys. Tell your dad we'll all be there to see him in May. That should cheer him up." "Will do." I said, and hung up the phone.

"Feel better?" mum said. "Yes, a little. Although I'm still angry. I'll sit down with him when I get back home." I was starting to feel more like myself again. I had always been so independent when I was married to John. Even when John passed away and I had Jessie to look after, I was in charge. But I seemed to have lost that with Frank. I should be able to ask him anything I wanted to know. Maybe subconsciously I didn't really want to know the answers. I had a lot of thinking to do.

My father was recovering well and Dr. Willson gave him a clean bill of health with a couple of warnings to take it easy for the next 6 weeks or so. Mum was ecstatic. She could have her man to look after again. It was so nice to see. My mother lived for my father even after all these years and he adored her. I wish my life was so clearly defined.

I headed home early Tuesday morning. My car was still at the airport so there was nobody there to greet me. I had some quiet time driving home to think.

As I drove into the driveway the front door opened and Frank and the boys were waiting for me. Did they anticipate my arrival or was it just co-incidence. Already I was becoming suspicious and I hadn't even entered the house. Once the boys hugged me and Frank kissed me, I turned into a marshmallow, again.

CHAPTER SEVENTY THREE

Frank had made soup and was in the process of making us grilled cheese sandwiches. I must admit, I was starving. I would eat first and ask questions later. The boys talked about the trip to the city and started showing me all the new clothes they had bought. "Try them on, let me see." I said. As they came out one by one in their new outfits I could see Frank wasn't paying much attention to the boys, he was watching me. I had changed. Neither the boys nor Frank mentioned their tests.

The rest of the day I spent on the phone with Mary, making sure everything was in order. "Great Mary, I said, I'll be in the office first thing in the morning, and thank you."

I was trying to be so cool but I think maybe I was trying too hard. I hadn't asked even one question about their so called tests. It felt like there was an elephant in the room that nobody wanted to acknowledge. Frank came up behind me and held me. "Angela, what's wrong?" "I'm really confused Frank. Your always in my head, you should know what's bothering me." I couldn't believe I just said that, neither could Frank. He backed away and turned me to face him. "Please Angela, spit it out, I need to know just what it is you think you know." "Well, maybe when the boys go to bed, we can go for a walk." I said as I looked him straight in the eye. "It's only four o'clock, I can't wait that long." Frank said. "I'm going to have a shower." I said, and walked into the bedroom.

I had never in my life started a confrontation but it would seem I would have to keep this one going if I were to live my life in peace with Frank. As I ran the shower Frank came into the bathroom. "I *promise*, I will answer any questions you have truthfully Angela, when you're ready to ask me." With that he turned and left the room. Now the ball was in my court and I really wasn't sure how to play the game.

Dinner time was a little strained. The boys didn't even argue about eating their peas and beans. That was enough to un-nerve me. They were always so animated at dinner time but not tonight. Frank just concentrated on eating his dinner and I just picked at my meal. I felt horrible. I'm sure Frank hadn't said anything to the boys, but they knew something was brewing and they looked worried. They kept looking at each other but not saying a word. Frank had given them the odd glance but hadn't said a word either. This was also part of what bothered me. It seemed as if they could communicate with each other without a word being said and I was an outsider. I would save that question for later.

Time is a funny thing, when you want it to go fast, it slows down. Tonight was no exception. When 7:30 came the boys automatically went to get their pyjamas on and came back into the living room where Frank and I sat in silence. I stood up to hug them. "You know mum, Frank Jr. said, we both love you unconditionally, honestly. You look so sad and we are worried you don't love us anymore." "How could you possibly think such a thing? I love you more than life itself." I said as I reached out to hold them.

It was a moment I would never forget. The boys were crying. I had never seen them cry before, not even as a baby and it broke my heart. Tears were falling down their beautiful faces and I felt like I had just beaten them. We held each other for a long time

Tea, Love & Suspicion

until the boys let me go. "Don't either of you worry that I could live without you, you mean the world to me."

I put the boys to bed for the first time in months. Without Frank. I kissed them goodnight and told them tomorrow was another day and I would make a special breakfast for them in the morning. "Love you mum." they said in unison. "Love you more." I said as I turned out the light. Now all I had to do was face Frank.

CHAPTER SEVENTY FOUR

Frank was waiting for me in the living room. I had brought my coat, it was cool outside and I planned on being out there until I had had all my questions answered.

"Are you ready for our walk?" I asked as I walked towards him. "Sure." he said. Maybe we can go sit in the park and talk." "Okay." I said as I walked towards the door. He already had his coat on so he *was* prepared to join me, for as long as it took. He opened the door and I stepped over the threshold in fear of what might be beyond. As we walked towards the park we didn't say a word. You could have cut the tension with a knife.

As we sat down on the park bench, Frank reached out and held my hand. "Before we discuss anything, I want to let you know one thing." He said. "I love you more than anything or anybody."

He shuffled around on the bench. "I'm so afraid that what you are about to hear may turn you against me but I am willing to take the risk so hopefully, I can have your unconditional love. So, ask your question my love. I will answer without reservation and I will take my chances that your love for me is greater than any of your concerns."

I looked at the troubled look on his face and my heart went out to him.

He held his head in his hands and bent over as if he were in great pain. I knew I had to ask him about so many things. I

Tea, Love & Suspicion 203

could leave well enough alone, but how could I? We could never be happy so long as I had so many doubts.

I wondered if he would really answer my questions truthfully.

But, where would I start? Maybe, if I started at the beginning. But where was the beginning. I remembered the first time I saw him and looked into those beautiful eyes. Yes, I thought, that was the beginning.

I wondered what I would do, if I didn't believe him. Or if what he had to say would make me flee.

CHAPTER SEVENTY FIVE

I took a deep breath. It was now or never.

"Frank." I blurted out. "I have had the feeling that when I got that flat tire on the back road, our meeting was planned."

"Was it?" I couldn't help but think that this was a really stupid question. How on earth could someone plan such an event? But I had asked the question. At least this really was the beginning.

He straightened up, looked me in the eye. "Yes." he said slowly.

How could that be I wondered? I had asked the question but the answer stunned me. I was about to ask another stupid question when the words just popped out of my mouth "Was this the first time we met?" I asked.

"No." he said as he held my hand again.

I searched my brain. I couldn't remember having met him before. He wasn't exactly the kind of man you would forget. "When was that? I don't remember even seeing you before then." I said. I was becoming more curious, I could hardly believe his answers but he had promised to be truthful.

"Do you remember the thunderstorm?" "Yes." I said. I could feel his grip tightening on my hands. "It was then." he said.

I couldn't believe it but in my muddled mind I was beginning to put things together. The missing hours during the thunderstorm. I hadn't thought about that for years.

No one other than George knew about that episode on my way to Jenna. I had never told another living sole. Except in the back of my mind I thought I remembered Frank mentioning it. I never told anyone because I thought people would just think I was crazy. How had he known about it? Now, I thought it was a question I *had* to ask, crazy or not. Everybody knew about these so called abductions. They were on the TV all the time. Was it really real? Maybe now I would find out just how crazy I was.

"What happened to me during the storm Frank?" I asked. Even though I really didn't want to know the answer. His voice cracked as he said. "We took you far away my love, to where I was born." I could feel the hairs on the back of my neck stand straight up. He stopped. As if he wanted to find the proper words. He went on.

"During the thunder storm, you did die. We had created the storm and you accidentally got caught in the middle of it. We meant no harm so we had to rescue you."

"You were brought to me."

"I was the one who breathed life back into you."

"From that moment on, I knew. Somehow I had to become part of your life. I set the plan in motion."

I sat there in disbelief. "I died?" This was almost more than I could take. Was my life real? Was it just a way to propagate? Did he really care anything about me? My mind was swimming. I got up off the bench and started walking in circles trying to think.

As I stood up I felt a surge come over me. As if I had just woken up. I looked over at Frank sitting on the bench. His eyes were searching mine looking for my response. Strangely enough, I felt stronger. Even though I had heard so many things I really wish I hadn't.

Since Frank had come back into my life I had felt like I had lost my independence. As I sat back down on the bench I looked into Franks' eyes. I could feel that power come back to me and I was ready for anything, well, almost anything.

CHAPTER SEVENTY SIX

Did I really want to know? Most definitely yes. If it meant keeping my boys, I felt I had no other choice.

I mustered all my strength as I sat beside him.

"I have just a few more questions for you Frank." I said as I sat straight up on the bench. I had control of myself again.

The flood gates had opened and I was ready.

"Frank," I said as I gripped his hands, "Do you really truly love me?"

There was no hesitation in his voice. "YES, more than life itself."

"Will you ever leave me?" "Never!" He said as he reached for my face and kissed me. I warmed to his touch but I still had so many un-answered questions. I backed away.

I could tell that he was uncomfortable answering all of my questions but I think he also knew that if he didn't, our lives would change dramatically. If I couldn't accept who, or what he was, we were in big trouble.

My boys were my prime concern now. I couldn't lose them. I knew if I lost Frank, I would lose the boys too.

I started to wonder where Frank and the boys were while I was away visiting my parents. If my father hadn't broken his hip, maybe I would have gone on for years in denial. Never knowing the truth.

I had come a long way while sitting on this bench. Strangely enough, I wasn't even afraid of the answers.

I calmly asked. "Where did you go with the boys?" He answered quickly. I think he knew I was ready to hear it all. "I took them to my home. They were ready for some answers too. They needed to know where their father was from and the window of opportunity came up. You have no idea, he said rather sheepishly, how badly I felt having to deceive you. Once I realized that I had been caught in a lie, I had to make myself ready for the consequences."

CHAPTER SEVENTY SEVEN

I was feeling the effect of the night air. I pulled my coat around me. Normally Frank and I would sit so close I wouldn't have felt the chill. But tonight was definitely different.

"I only have two more questions for you Frank although I am sure I will think of many more after this night is over. Tonight was just the beginning. It felt like I had opened Pandora's Box.

My throat was dry and I was having trouble getting my words out.

"Are you and the boys the only ones?" "No." he said, as he reached for my hand. "There are thousands more, maybe even millions. You met two, not long ago." He paused. "Simon."

"Oh my God." I said. "Are all of you so attractive?" I couldn't believe those words came out of my mouth. "Who was the other?" "I'm sure you remember Tara." "Good grief, Mr. and Mrs. perfect." Frank couldn't help but smile. "Well." He said. "I suppose it doesn't hurt to be attractive. People are much more trusting of attractive people. It makes it easier for us to fit in."

I couldn't believe it but I was beginning to accept Frank for who, or what he was. I stood up and looked down on him. "My last and most important question probably means the most."

"Do you mean any harm to us here on earth?" He stood up and put his arms around me. "No!" he said. He said it with such conviction, I truly believed him.

"Do you have anything else to ask me?" He said. "No, not at the moment, I said, although I'm sure I'll think of something else tomorrow." "Will you still answer me truthfully?" "Yes." he said. "We have no more secrets."

Maybe tomorrow I could ask him why they were here but I had had enough for one night. I was exhausted.

"I have just one important question for you Angela. You have heard so much tonight, you don't have to answer straight away, you can take your time."

I could see he was agonizing over the question. How difficult could it be after all we had been through tonight?

He held my hands. "After all of this Angela do you love me, in spite of everything you know?"

I reached up, took his face in my hands and brought his lips to mine. "I do love you Frank, maybe more now than I ever did before." We kissed and held each other until we heard the boys.

It was as if on cue again. Harry and Frank Jr. came running towards us in their pyjamas and threw their arms around both of us. Frank put his hand on my belly and whispered in my ear. I smiled and kissed him.

We put our arms around our boys and headed towards the house. Now I could live in peace and their secret was safe with me.

Besides, let's face it, who would ever believe me......

CPSIA information can be obtained at www.ICGtesting.com
Printed in the USA
LVOW11*1315301113

363246LV00001B/3/P